keeper

COLETTE MCCORMICK

Published by Accent Press Ltd 2019
Octavo House
West Bute Street
Cardiff
CF10 5LJ

www.accentpress.co.uk

ISBN 9781786156532
eISBN 9781786156549

Printed and bound in Great Britain by Clays Ltd,
Elcograf S.p.A

PROLOGUE

As brothers went, there wasn't much to distinguish Robert and Tom Ellis from any other set of brothers that had gone before them or since.

With a little over two years between them, they grew up playing together, learning together, and even occasionally fighting together. As little boys they were each other's best friend.

As older boys the bond of brotherhood – though still strong – became stretched as new friendships were formed. By the time they were both at secondary school, they were brothers who looked out for each other's welfare, though they had little in common.

As adolescents, when raging hormones turned cherubs into demons, the stretched bond strengthened again; they were two boys standing together against parents who had forgotten what it was like to be young.

As young men, they established who they really were.

ROBERT

I don't know what you want me to say. I was just a normal kid.

I liked my mates, I loved football and I hated school.

The only thing that I liked about school was the break times, which I spent either playing footie with my mates or round the back of the gym doing whatever the girl I was with would allow me to. My kid brother was the academic one in the family and more than one teacher said that I should take a leaf out of his book. No chance. The only lesson I liked was the one that Mr Dawson taught in car mechanics but it wasn't really a lesson at all, more of a hobby class really; a bit like chess club.

My best mate at school was a lad called Craig Jenkins. We started on the same day and were in the same class all the way through. He was a massive lad – wide as well as tall – and he liked school even less than I did. We sometimes used to wag off and go into town together. He had a sister called Michelle who was in our Tom's year. I think they did Maths together.

Me and Craig lost touch a bit after we left school. He got a job on a building site and I started working for Bill Deardon who had a garage behind North Road. We made new friends and didn't have the common bond of hating school anymore. I still saw him sometimes when I was out, especially if I was in the Big Tree on a Friday night, but we weren't as close as we had been.

I loved my job. I mean, I know I spent the first six months making tea and watching what the other mechanics did, but Bill said that that was the way I would learn. I think I'd been there almost a year before I got my hands on anything under the bonnet of a car but I had learned a lot from watching the others and Bill was pleased with what I could do.

I came across Craig's sister again in the summer of 1980 when I was twenty years old. I was in The Queens Head on Station Street one Saturday night when I saw our Tom in the corner with one of his mates. They were sitting there sipping their pints when I saw a young, blonde lass go up to him and start talking. Tom said something to her and she laughed. I had no idea who she was but, even seeing her from behind, I could tell that I wanted to find out.

I'd been sitting at the bar waiting for Tony, one of the lads I worked with, but I thought *sod Tony* and slid off the stool. I grabbed my pint and made my way through the crowd.

'You all right, Tom?' I asked, though I didn't even look at him or the lad he was sitting with. I was looking at the girl. There was something familiar about her but I couldn't put my finger on it; I couldn't place her. It was obvious that she could tell I was trying to work out who she was because a little smile curled only half her lip, as though she was enjoying my struggle.

'You remember Michelle, don't you,' Tim said eventually. 'You know, Craig's sister.'

Bloody hell she'd changed! I mean she'd always had a pretty enough face but the last time I'd seen her she was still gawky in that fourteen-year-old kid sort of way. She was anything but gawky now.

I tried to sound casual as I said, ''Course I do,' but anyone could tell that I was lying. 'How are you doing, Michelle?' I asked.

'I'm fine thanks, Robert.' She lowered her eyes as she spoke and I knew right then that I'd be walking her home that night.

I did walk her home that night, and the one after that, and before long we were a couple. After a few weeks I even took her home, which my mum said must make it serious. I didn't know about that, but Michelle had said she wanted to meet my parents and I thought why not? Dad liked her but Mum didn't seem so sure. She was pleasant enough to Michelle but I couldn't help feeling her heart wasn't in it. If Michelle noticed it she was too polite to say.

It was the same thing in reverse when I met her parents. I went over for my tea one Saturday night and Michelle's mother was all over me like a rash – would you like more potatoes, Robert, have you got enough chicken, Robert? – that sort of thing. Her dad looked at me out of the corner of his eye as he ate his food and asked me what I did for a living. I felt as though he was weighing up my prospects.

Craig wasn't there the first time I went to the house, but when he was there on other occasions he acted a bit like his dad. I thought it was strange because he knew me, but maybe that was why he was suspicious of my intentions. He only had one sister and even when we were kids it was obvious he would have done anything for her. There was one time, just after Tom and Michelle had started secondary school, when one of the fifth years came on to Michelle and teased her about the size of her non-existent breasts. Craig heard about it and threatened that if the lad ever so much as spoke to his sister again he'd regret it. Even though he was two years younger, Craig was already bigger than the fifth year and twice as menacing. As far as I know, Michelle didn't receive unwanted attention after that.

Luckily for me, Michelle wanted mine.

She was a lovely girl and I liked her a lot but I couldn't help realising she wanted more. I just wanted something casual; she wanted me to tell her that I loved her. And eventually I told her I did simply because I knew it was what she wanted to hear.

At that point, we hadn't slept together – she'd said she wanted to save herself for the right person. But, as far as she was concerned, I now loved her, so that made me the right person. I took her virginity in the back of a Mini Clubman Estate that I'd parked behind the old ironworks. She cried.

I did want to love her but it just wasn't in me; it wasn't in me to love anyone. I was twenty one years old and much too young for any of that crap.

Soon, my telling her that I loved her wasn't enough and every other week she told me about some friend or other

6

that was getting engaged. One of them even got married.

My twenty second birthday was at the beginning of February, and Michelle said she had a special birthday present for me. I met her at the hospital gate just after eight o'clock – she was training to be a nurse and had a placement at the General Hospital. I saw her come out of a door with a couple of other people but she said goodbye to them quickly and came trotting over to me. She was wearing a Trench coat tied tightly at the waist and her collar was turned up against the cold. I'd been wondering all day what this special birthday present could be and – it sounds daft now – as I watched her coming towards me I hoped it involved her being naked underneath her coat.

It didn't.

To be fair to her, I think she actually believed I'd be happy to hear her say it.

'Robert, I'm pregnant.'

I wasn't.

TOM

I was two years and four days younger than him, and when I was a child, my brother Robert was my hero. He was confident and outgoing; he was popular and had loads of friends. He was everything that I wasn't.

He'd left school as soon as he finished his O Levels and got a job as a mechanic in a back-street garage. Mum wasn't very happy about that because she said he should have stopped on at school and done better for himself. The trouble was that he didn't want to better himself – he was happy with the way he was. That was one of the things that I loved the most about Robert; he knew who he was and he was happy with it.

Me? I hadn't a clue who I was.

I left school after my O Levels too but I didn't get a job. When I was sixteen I wasn't ready for the real world. The real world terrified me. I enrolled in art college with the hope of doing God knows what. Mum and Dad would have preferred me to stay on at school but they seemed pleased that I was at least furthering my education.

'Don't know what good it'll do you,' my dad said when I told him what I was doing – he didn't think of art as a real subject. If I'm honest, I probably agreed with him but, like I said, I just wasn't ready for reality.

I met my first girlfriend at college, a girl called Carol-Anne Dempsey. She was a petite brunette with long eyelashes and a very loud laugh. We spent a couple of months together in the summer of '79 before she gave me the elbow. When I realised that I wasn't bothered, I decided she'd done me a favour. That laugh really did grate on you after a bit.

By that time, I had nothing in common with Robert other than our shared parentage. Pretty much the only thing we ever did together was be in the same pub on a Friday night occasionally. I'd see Robert at the bar, laughing with his mates and chatting up girls and, God help me, despite everything I couldn't help admiring him. Once someone caught me looking at him and asked me who he was.

'That's my brother,' I said and even I could hear the pride in my voice.

I never heard anyone say that he talked about me in the same way.

This thing between me and Robert started when I was with my mate Alan in that pub at the top of Station Street one Friday night in 1980. I couldn't tell you exactly when but I know it was summer because it was still light well into the evening. Anyway, we were just sitting there minding our own business when I heard someone say my name. I turned around and saw a blonde girl standing beside me.

'I knew it was you,' she said. 'I haven't seen you in ages. How are you? What are doing to these days?'

I recognised her instantly. Michelle Jenkins wasn't the sort of girl that you forget. Like every other lad in our year I'd admired her from afar when were at school but I hadn't seen her since we'd left. Her face was the same as it had always been but in the intervening years her body had developed and changed her from a skinny kid into a curvy woman.

I said that I was fine and asked how she was and what she was up to. She told me she was training to be a nurse, which impressed me no end.

We chatted for a few minutes about nothing specific and I was about to ask her if I could buy her a drink when, out of the blue, our Robert appeared. He asked me if I was all right but he didn't even look at me: he only had eyes for Michelle.

I can't even tell you how pissed off I was by that. Robert had nodded a greeting when he'd come in about an hour earlier but he hadn't shown the slightest bit of interest in me since then. Until he saw a pretty girl talking to me that is – then he was there like a rat up a drainpipe.

I didn't blame Michelle for giving her attention to Robert rather than me. It's just the way it always was. I was used to it – but it didn't make it any easier to stomach.

As I watched them walk away together I finished my pint and told Alan that I'd had enough and was going home. By the time I got outside, Robert and Michelle were climbing into the back seat of a taxi.

I was surprised when Robert brought Michelle home for tea; I couldn't think of any other girl he'd brought home before. Dad was OK but Mum sort of glared at her all the way through whatever we were eating. Mum wasn't much of a cook so, whatever it was, I'm sure Michelle was underwhelmed. Mum made some effort and was perfectly polite but you could just tell that it wasn't genuine. Dad seemed to like Michelle though and they chatted together quite easily. I didn't stay long. I just ate as much as I could get away with and then made an excuse that I had somewhere to be.

I couldn't quite get my head around them as a couple and I wasn't sure of the reason why. I think it was jealousy.

Of what, you ask – of Robert, of course – he'd had the confidence to just walk up to Michelle and start talking, whereas I'd fumbled through asking her what she was doing for a living. She hadn't taken a lot of persuading to turn her attention to him but I didn't hold it against her. Robert was a catch, people were always telling me so.

ROBERT

I just looked at her and stuttered, 'Are you sure?'

I hoped that she'd start laughing and tell me she was joking but she didn't. She just looked at me with those big eyes of hers and nodded her head, slowly.

A couple of girls walked past us and shouted things like, 'goodnight' and 'see you tomorrow,' to Michelle. She looked at them but didn't say anything. Then she looked back at me, but I still didn't have anything to say to her.

I didn't know *what* to say.

She asked me what I was thinking.

I was thinking *how the hell could you be pregnant?* But I knew that wasn't what she wanted to hear. I was asking myself how it could have happened. Had she forgotten to take her pill? I was wondering what she would want to do, what she would want me to do.

'Robert?'

I looked at her and saw that tears had formed and were pooling at the edges of her eyes.

'What are you thinking?'

All I could do was look at her.

She looked away and sucked in a deep breath which she let out in stages. Her hand was shaking as she brought it up to her cheeks and brushed away a tear that had escaped. 'What are we going to do?' she asked as she sniffed.

'I don't know,' I said, finally. 'What do you want to

do?'

'I want to go home,' she said, brushing my arm as she walked past me.

I went after her of course, I wasn't going to let her walk home on her own but we didn't say anything else, not a word. Occasionally I felt her looking at me as I looked at my feet.

I walked her to the door of her parents' house. She had her hand on the door knob and was about to turn it when I touched her arm. She turned around and looked at me.

'Don't worry,' I told her. 'Everything will be all right.'

Even as I said the words I didn't believe what I was saying. How *could* everything be all right? I didn't want a kid. I wasn't even sure that I wanted Michelle anymore.

I hardly slept a wink that night and spent most of the time lying on my back looking at the ceiling. I wondered if Michelle was doing the same.

I wondered, too, about how long Michelle had known, how far along she was and would she want to keep it? Surely she wasn't any more ready to be a parent than I was; she wasn't even twenty years old yet. It occurred to me that she might be able to get something from the hospital – you know, some potion or other that she could take that would make the problem go away – but I doubted that she would have taken it even if such a thing had existed. Perhaps she'd consider adoption but I doubted that too so I guessed she was going to be a parent whether she was ready or not.

At some point during the night I wondered if she had

told her parents but I thought that she probably hadn't, because if she had, their Craig would have been round to tell me when I had to be at the altar.

The altar.

That was when it hit me. Michelle would want to get married.

Shit! The word echoed around my head and I remember covering my eyes with my hands, forcing my fingertips into the sockets.

I spent the rest of the night lying on one side and then the other in the hope that I could get at least a little sleep, though I spent half the time looking at a wall and the rest of it looking at the clock.

Eventually I came up with a plan.

Mum was in the kitchen when I went downstairs the following morning.

'You all right, love?' she asked in that chirpy way she always had in the mornings. She was making packed lunches, just like she did every morning, one for my dad and one for me. I mustn't have answered her quickly enough because she asked the question again.

'I'm fine,' I snapped. 'Why wouldn't I be?'

She asked me what I wanted for breakfast, the choice was probably toast or cereal, neither of which I was that keen on but I usually managed to choke at least one of them down. I couldn't face food that morning so I told her that I had to get to work early. She handed me the box that she'd just filled with my lunch and I took it, not because I wanted it but because I couldn't be bothered with the inquisition that would follow if I didn't. Food was the last thing on my mind but my mother didn't need to know why.

I spent most of the first hour at work lying on a trolley underneath a Ford Escort that had a dodgy crank shaft. After the first ten minutes I stopped even bothering to pretend to fix it and lay there thinking. I'd spent the past fifteen hours thinking. There was a radio playing in the background and the hum of conversation but none of that concerned me.

I hadn't noticed that there was anyone anywhere near me until I heard Brian, one of the other mechanics, say, 'I know mate. But divorce?'

'It's the only way,' came the reply, in Martin's thick, Glaswegian accent.

I held my breath and listened. I wasn't sure who would have been more embarrassed if they'd realised that I was nearby.

'How long have you been married?' Brian asked, and Martin said that it had been ten years. Neither of them said anything for a few seconds and then Brian asked him why. Someone, Martin presumably, let out a long sigh. 'We were too young,' he said, 'and she was pregnant.'

They walked away a few minutes later and I stayed where I was for a good ten minutes after that.

When Bill asked if anyone was free to go and pick up a carburettor that hadn't been delivered I got in there before anyone else had a chance. I'd made a decision during the night and while I was under that Ford Escort I knew that I was going to have to put it into action before I lost my bottle.

I never made it to the suppliers and I didn't pick up the carburettor. About four hours later I wondered if Bill had realised that I wasn't coming back.

After I left work I drove straight home with only one thing on my mind. I took the stairs two at a time and crossed the landing as quickly as I could. I opened the door to my bedroom and grabbed the bag from the top of my wardrobe. The doors were already open so I grabbed whatever I could and stuffed it into the bag. I wasn't really aware of what I was picking up, just blindly getting handfuls of this and that. Whatever I forgot I'd have to buy when I got where I was going.

When the bag was full, I zipped it up, had one last look around and left the room. I closed the door behind me.

I don't mind telling you that I was sweating bricks as I leaned against the door, and I could feel my heart pounding in my chest. I remember puffing out my cheeks as I breathed.

I dropped the bag by my feet, reached into the back pocket of my jeans and pulled out three envelopes containing the letters that I had written in the early hours of the morning when I'd finally given up on sleep. I'd known it would come to this, I just hadn't known when. I hadn't known that the first chance I got would be so soon, but the opportunity was too good to miss. I just had to do it.

I looked at the envelope on the top. I left the bag where I had dropped it and moved to the door next to the one that I had just closed. I stood a second or two with my hand resting on the handle and after a deep intake of breath I twisted it and opened the door to Tom's bedroom.

It had been my intention to keep my head down and be in and out of there as quickly as I could but as soon as I opened the door my eyes were drawn to the shelves that ran along the length of one wall. I had to laugh when I saw a collection of books standing neatly on one of the shelves because, since he'd left school, I had never seen Tom read a book. He might have read a newspaper now and then but that was it. Next to the books was the tribe of apaches that had been Tom's pride and joy when we were young and we used to play with the fort that Dad had made us. I knew for a fact that I'd long since thrown the cavalry in the bin but I'd be willing to bet that if I looked in one of Tom's cupboards I would still find the fort.

He always was a sentimental sod.

Anyway, I didn't have time for all of our yesterdays so I took the envelope that was at the top of the pile and moved towards the table beside the bed. I could see my hand shaking as it hovered over it. It felt like the envelope was glued to my hand and I struggled to let it go. But something else attracted my attention and I dropped the envelope so that I could pick it up. It was a red photograph frame containing a picture of the two of us on Christmas morning about ten years earlier. We were sitting on the bikes that we had received that morning and were smiling at the camera.

We'd not had a care in the world.

Tom probably still didn't, but I felt like there was a massive weight sitting on my shoulders. Before I knew what I was doing I'd flipped the frame over, unclipped the back and slipped the photograph into my pocket. I put the empty frame back on the table and left the room as quickly as I could. I don't know if I even bothered to close Tom's door, I just wanted to get out of there. I could feel my resolve starting to falter and I knew that I needed to do what I had to as quickly as possible.

After I'd left Tom's room I picked up the bag I'd left on the landing and walked down the stairs. I'd gone up them two at a time but, despite what I've just told you about needing to hurry, I went down the stairs much more slowly.

I left the second envelope, the one with the words 'Mum and Dad' written on it, on the telephone table that sat in the hallway. I caught sight of my reflection in the mirror that hung on the wall above and stared at it. I could see the muscles around my jaw twitch as I clenched my teeth together. I had a haunted look on my face – was it any bloody wonder?

As I left the house that had been the only home I had ever known, I couldn't help asking myself if I was doing the right thing. There was still time to change my mind. I could go back in and collect the envelopes I'd left. I could put the things that I had taken back. I could do things differently.

But I didn't.

I drove the short distance to Michelle's house and pulled the car up to the kerb. I turned the engine off and sat behind the wheel for a second or two before I got out the car and took the final envelope from my pocket. It wasn't just my hands that were shaking now, it was my legs as well. I felt them buckle a bit as I took the first step.

Once again, I questioned my actions. Was I really that pathetic? Was I really such a bastard?

The answer was obviously yes, because I practically ran to the door and pushed the envelope through the letter box. I spared a second to look up at Michelle's bedroom window before I got back in the car and drove away. I wasn't proud of what I was doing but I did it nonetheless.

I'm not ashamed to tell you that when I'd hatched this plan in the wee small hours I'd cried because I was sad. As I drove away, I cried again, not through sadness this time but through fear. Not because I didn't know where I was going, but because I was bloody terrified of the type of man that my actions meant I was.

I brushed away a tear or two as I went down the slip road and joined the motorway.

TOM

I'll never forget the day that Robert left. It was the day after his twenty second birthday.

We were a bit like ships that passed in the night but we normally exchanged grunts over breakfast except there was just Mum in the kitchen that morning. I wasn't surprised that Dad wasn't there because he usually left early for work but it was unusual not to see Robert sitting at the table shoving food into his mouth. I remember asking Mum where he was.

'He had to go to work early,' she said though she didn't sound like she believed it and I know I didn't. He never went to the garage a minute earlier than he had to, and he was always home within ten minutes of the garage closing at five. I should have known then that there was something wrong.

'Did you hear him during the night?' Mum asked as she handed me a plate that had a couple of slices of toast on it. I told her I hadn't. 'He was tossing and turning all night,' she said. She went back to drying dishes but I could see that she was doing it on autopilot. She was looking out of the window for a start, which was pointless: there wasn't anything to see out there because it was still dark. It was just somewhere to look.

I tried telling her not to worry. 'He's probably just had a row with Michelle,' I said.

'No, no, it's not that, I'm sure of it,' she said, still rubbing the same plate.

I didn't know what to say so I thought it best to keep quiet. I kept my head down and ate the toast. It wasn't much of a breakfast, but then I'm not much of a breakfast person so it did for me. I put the last of the toast in my mouth, chewed, and swallowed it as quickly as I could. I took the plate to the sink and dropped it into the water. Mum was bent over so I kissed the top of her head and told her one last time not to worry. 'He'll be fine,' I said, but I could see that my words did nothing to convince her.

I know that by that point Robert and I weren't as close as we had been but I still spared a thought for him during the day. I wondered what could have kept him tossing and turning through the night. I'd never known him to worry about a thing in all of his life so I couldn't imagine what would stop him sleeping. I know I'd said that he might have had a row with Michelle but I didn't even believe the words myself. He wouldn't have lost any sleep over that. He wasn't the type to get upset over rowing with a girlfriend. God knows he'd had plenty of practice.

I got home just before half four and nearly fell over the three bags of shopping that were sitting in the hallway. I picked them up and carried them to the kitchen. Mum was sitting at the table and I asked her if she was all right as I put the bags on the work bench. It was a bloody silly question given that she'd left shopping by the front door and was sitting at the table staring at whatever it was that she was holding in her hands. She didn't answer me.

I looked at her but she didn't move, not even an eyelid as far as I could tell. I sat on the chair next to her and asked her the question again. She was still staring at her hands. I glanced at them and saw that she was holding an envelope. I put my hand on her arm just above her wrist and asked her the question for a third time.

Slowly she dragged her eyes away from the envelope and looked at me. Her eyes were wide and a little bit wild and to be honest she didn't look like my mother at all.

I could hear the tremble in my voice as I asked, 'Mum, what's wrong?'

As her eyes went back to the envelope I noticed that her hands were shaking. I'll be honest, by that point I was getting a bit worried and I wished with all my heart that Robert or my dad would come in so that I didn't have to deal with whatever was happening to Mum on my own.

'What's that?' I asked. 'What's in the envelope?' She still didn't answer me so I pressed her and asked, 'Who's it from? Is it Dad?'

I don't know why I asked that last bit, why I thought it was Dad. I suppose I thought it was the only thing that could have caused such a reaction. Anyway, it worked, because at least it made her speak.

'No,' she croaked, 'it's not your dad.' As she looked at me I could see that her eyes were puffy and almost closed through the tears she had obviously been crying, probably for hours. She put the envelope on the table and pushed it towards me. She pulled her hands back quickly and tucked them into her chest. 'It's from Robert,' she whispered.

'Robert?' I looked from her to the envelope and back again. 'Why?'

She mouthed the words, 'I don't know,' but the sound never made it out of her mouth. She made such a pitiful sight it almost broke my heart.

'What does it say?' I really couldn't get my head around what was happening or what she was telling me. Why would Robert be writing her a letter?

Mum tried to say the words again but nothing came out that time either.

'Why haven't you read it, Mum?' I asked gently.

She brushed more tears away and said, 'Because I'm scared.'

'Scared?' I wasn't trying to be clever I just really didn't understand but I couldn't help noticing that it sounded like I was being sarcastic.

'Yes, scared,' she snapped, suddenly finding her voice, though the fight in her was gone as quickly as it had arrived. 'I knew there was something wrong with him this morning and now this,' she gestured towards the letter that was still sitting on the table.

'Do you want me to read it?' I asked.

As she nodded her head slowly, more tears rolled down her cheeks.

Dad came home from work at some point and found me and Mum still sitting at the kitchen table. I was holding Mum's hand and two envelopes sat on the table in front of us. There was the one marked 'Mum and Dad' which Mum had been holding when I found her, and another one addressed to 'Tommo'. Tommo was me – or rather it used to be me; it's what the family had called me when I was small. I had found the letter on my bedside table.

'What's going on?' Dad asked as he took his jacket off and hung it on the back of the door. He looked at his wife and then he looked at me. 'What's wrong Tom? What's wrong with your mum?' I could hear the concern in his voice. God knows what he must have thought was happening. He caught sight of the envelopes on the table and asked. 'What are they?'

'Robert's gone,' I said hoarsely.

'Gone? What do you mean gone?' He was as confused as I'd been. I pushed the first letter towards him and told him that he'd better sit down.

He looked at Mum as he pulled the chair out and sat down but she was looking straight ahead at the wall that the cooker sat against. He looked at me as he picked up the envelope addressed to him and Mum and I tried to force a smile but I don't think I pulled it off. He picked it up and turned it over like he was looking for a clue. When he couldn't find one he took the single sheet of paper out and read the letter silently. I'd read it a dozen times and I can still tell you exactly what it said.

Dear Mum and Dad
I love you both. Thanks for everything, you were great.
Look after each other.
Robert

'What's this?' Dad asked. He looked at me first and then at my mother. 'What's this all about, Janet?'

At the mention of her name, Mum's resolve finally crumbled and she let go of me so that she could bury her face deep into her hands. As she sobbed, her shoulders moved up and down and something resembling an animal noise came out of her mouth. Dad was around the table in seconds, kneeling next to his wife and enveloping her in his arms. He was whispering something to her and stroking her hair as he gently rocked her from side to side. I felt a bit like I was intruding in an intimate moment but I didn't know how to leave. So I stayed where I was and felt awkward.

After a few minutes Mum was calm enough for Dad to loosen his hold on her and stand up. He was still stroking her hair as he turned to me and asked me what was going on.

'Michelle's pregnant,' I told him.

I could see from the look on his face that he was still confused, but then the penny dropped the reality hitting him was visible in his eyes.

'And he's buggered off?' He phrased it like a question, like maybe he'd got the wrong end of the stick.

'Yeah,' I said but I couldn't maintain the eye contact. As I looked at the table I could hear Mum gently crying beside me.

'This doesn't say anything about Michelle being pregnant,' he said as he threw the letter on to the table.

'No, but this one does.' I pushed the envelope addressed to me towards him. I'd discovered the note when I'd gone upstairs to check on Mum. She'd said that she needed the bathroom but when she hadn't come back after ten minutes I'd gone after her. She'd chosen the moment my foot touched the top step to open the bathroom door so I'd made the excuse that I wanted to change my shirt and gone into my bedroom while she went downstairs.

I'd noticed that the door to my room was slightly open which spiked my curiosity because I was certain that I'd closed it that morning. Who'd been in there? I'd pushed the door gently and it had swung open. Everything had looked as it usually did and I thought maybe I hadn't closed the door that morning after all. But then my gaze fell on the bedside table where the photograph frame was lying face down. When I'd lifted it up, the back had fallen off and the frame was empty. *What the hell?* As the question went through my head, my eyes fell on the envelope with 'Tommo' written on it.

As I read the note, things started to fall into place, though I didn't know what to make of the missing photograph.

Before I'd gone back downstairs I'd stuck my head into Robert's room and seen that the wardrobe doors were open. The canvas bag that normally sat on top of the wardrobe was missing, as were most of his clothes.

I'd gone back to the kitchen and found Mum back at the table. She'd looked up as I'd gone in but her eyes were drawn to the letter I was holding. She'd opened her mouth to speak, but only managed the word, 'Is …?'

'Yes,' I'd said and handed it to her. She'd read it and now Dad was doing the same.

It was longer than the brief note Robert had addressed to our parents but I can still remember every word.

Tommo,

I'm not much of a letter writer so I'm going to make this short and sweet. Michelle's pregnant and I don't know what to do. I'm not ready to be a dad, I don't want to be one, and I definitely don't want to be a husband – not to Michelle or anyone else. I know I'm a complete shit but I'm just trying to be honest.

I'm sorry for all the crap I'll be leaving you to deal with but I'm leaving anyway.

Look after Mum and Dad and watch out for Michelle if you get the chance.

Robert

Dad took a long time reading the letter. I think he might have read it twice just in case he hadn't understood it properly the first time. Then he put the letter back in the envelope and tossed it on the table.

'Bastard.' He spat the word out.

'Bob!' Mum was horrified.

I'd never heard Dad swear before and I tried to keep my surprise at his language off my face.

'No, Janet,' he said with a defiant look in his eyes, 'he's my son and I love him but if he's doing this,' he waved his hand towards the letter, 'then he's a bastard.' He started to pace the floor. 'He gets a lass pregnant and then he runs away from his responsibilities? I thought I'd brought my lads up better than that.' He looked towards my mother whose sobs had returned. 'Save your tears, Janet,' he said. 'He's not worth it.'

'He's our son,' Mum wailed.

'Not anymore,' Dad said and it was obvious that he was struggling to control his emotions.

'Don't say that, Bob,' Mum cried but it was too late. Dad had left the room.

Mum left the kitchen shortly after that too. She said she was going to have a lie down.

I followed her and watched as she slowly climbed the stairs. It looked like she was carrying a heavy weight on each foot. I saw Dad standing in the living room looking out of the window. I opened the front door and left the house as quietly as I could. I silently cursed Robert for leaving me to deal with his 'crap'.

I saw the curtains twitch as I opened the gate and the door was open before I had chance to ring the bell.

Michelle stood there, her eyes swollen with tears, and I knew that in the dim light she had mistaken me for someone else, someone she wanted to see. She had thought I was Robert. Disappointment was written all over her face.

As we stood looking at each other, a shadow appeared at her shoulder and a voice said, 'What do you want? Has he sent you?'

Craig Jenkins, the huge child that had terrorised half the kids in school, had grown into a truly huge man. For the first time I felt the terror that the other kids had felt. As the brother of his best mate I'd been safe in the school yard, but I doubted that would be the case now. Craig would probably kick my head in just because I was Robert's brother. It's what I would have done if someone had treated my sister the way Robert had. If I couldn't have got to the one who was responsible, I think I might have gone for the next best thing. I remember making a conscious decision that if he did decide to pummel me, I'd take the beating. I'd just let him get on with it. Hopefully it wouldn't come to that but it was good to have a plan.

'Come in, Tom.' Michelle stood to one side as she invited me in.

'What are you doing, Michelle?' Craig was whispering but he might as well have screamed at her, and his words couldn't have been more menacing if he had.

There was defiance as well as sadness as she looked at her brother and that was enough for him to back down. Craig disappeared into the house and Michelle opened the door even further.

There was a light on in a room off the hallway but the rest of the house was in darkness.

'Come in,' Michelle said, leading the way to the back of the house. As I followed her I noticed her parents in the only lit room. I saw her dad stand up only to be pulled back down by his wife. I turned my head away quickly. Michelle had put the light on in the kitchen by then and was waiting for me. After she closed the door behind us she turned around slowly and crossed her arms over her chest. Her eyes were flitting around, looking at me and then away. Her lips were trembling.

'Where is he?' she asked. The tremble was in her voice as well as her lips and she sounded like she was going to burst into tears at any minute. I didn't know if I'd be able to stand it if she started crying.

'I don't know,' I told her.

Obviously, that wasn't what she had wanted to hear and it was enough to push her over the edge. She lost control of the composure she'd been trying to hang on to and started crying.

For the love of God, I thought to myself. *What am I supposed to do now?* I took a step towards her, though God only knew why, and I was grateful when she held her hand up to tell me to stay where I was. She pulled out a chair and fell onto it. I didn't know what else to do so I pulled out the chair beside her and sat down. I watched her and waited for her to give me a clue as to what I should do.

She gave a hard sniff and wiped her nose with the back of her hand. 'Where is he?' she asked again.

As I looked at her all I could think was *how could you do this to her, Robert?* Surely he'd realised that she would react this way. But then, if he had he wouldn't have left her like this... would he? That was when I gave myself a mental slap around the head because of course he would. I've told you how much I loved my brother, idolised him even, but that didn't blind me to his faults.

Robert would have known fine well that this was how Michelle would react. What other way was there? She was twenty years old, pregnant, and deserted by a man she probably thought loved her. Of course she'd be bawling her eyes out and wondering where he was. But none of that would have mattered to him. These days Robert only did what was best for Robert.

'Stop it,' I told her. Either she hadn't heard me or she was choosing to ignore me because she carried on crying.

'Stop it,' I said again, only louder this time, loud enough to get her to look at me. I stood up and grabbed a handful of tissues out of the box that sat on the bench. The box was almost empty and it occurred to me that if the box had been full earlier in the afternoon, she'd wasted a lot of tears. I offered her the tissues as I sat back down. She took them from me, separated one from the bunch and blew her nose.

'He left me a note,' she said with a sniff. She was looking down at the table as she spoke and gravity moved her tears down her cheeks and off the end of her chin. I realise it was a stupid thing that went through my head but I thought that my mother had looked cheerful by comparison. Finally, Michelle lifted her head. 'Mum found it when she got home,' she said before she sniffed again.

'What time was that?' I asked.

'About twelve I think.' She looked puzzled. 'Why?'

I told her I was just curious but the reality was that I was trying to work out how long he had been gone. If he had left Michelle's note some time before twelve, and assuming that he had gone straight away, that meant that he had been on the road for at least seven hours. But maybe he'd dropped her letter off first and then left from home. That would make a difference of, what, half an hour at most? My best guess was that he'd been gone at least six and a half hours. He could have got a long way in six and a half hours. It was a waste of time wondering about it really, because we would only know the actual sequence of events when Robert came back and explained everything. If he came back at all.

Michelle and I sat in silence for a few minutes. She was crying and she dabbed her eyes or her nose from time to time. I sat with my head down feeling like a spare part. After a while, Michelle reached into the back pocket of her jeans and pulled out the note Robert had left her. It was crumpled into a ball and she chucked it onto the table vaguely in my direction. I wasn't sure what I was supposed to do. Did she want me to read it? I thought she must or why else would she have thrown it at me?

'Can I?' I asked, though I really didn't want to. I'd already seen more than enough of my brother's handwriting that day. She nodded her head so I reluctantly picked it up and tried to straighten the paper out. I flattened it out on the table.

Like the others, that note is etched forever on my brain, like that speech from *Richard III* that Mrs Wilkinson made us all learn in English.

Chelle, it said, which made me even more

uncomfortable if such a thing were possible. Obviously that was his pet name for her. How could he use her pet name when he was shitting all over her? Anyway, *Chelle*, it said, *I'm sorry. I don't know what else to say. You're better off without me. Bobby.*

Bobby? Bobby? Who the hell called him Bobby? Well clearly Chelle did.

I didn't doubt that she was better off without the selfish bastard but that still didn't make it the right thing to do.

I handed the note back to her. She took a deep breath and puffed out her cheeks to blow it out. 'I'm going to have to tell them, aren't I?' she said.

Tell them? I thought, *tell them what?*

'They think I'm just really upset because Robert's packed me in,' she explained and I noticed that she hadn't called him Bobby. 'My dad said that there are plenty more fish in the sea.' She gave a tiny little laugh when she said that. 'They have no idea.' She didn't laugh that time. There were just more tears rolling down her cheeks.

When I finally realised that she hadn't told her family about the baby, I asked, 'Do you want me to stay?'

I left about half an hour later. Michelle tried to smile at me when she saw me to the door but she wasn't fooling anyone.

Mum and Dad were both in the living room when I got home. The television was on but neither of them was watching it. Mum was staring into space and Dad was pretending to read the paper.

Have you ever seen those nature programmes where a meerkat hears a noise and it becomes alert, looking around to see where the noise came from? Well Mum was like that when the phone rang. Her head turned towards the telephone and she started to push herself out of her chair. It was obvious who she hoped it would be but I thought she'd suffered enough that day so I put my hand on her shoulder and told her that I'd get it. I thought that the chances of it being Robert were almost nil.

I lifted the receiver to my ear and said, 'Hello?'

'Is he there?' I recognised Michelle's voice. I'd half expected it to be her and I wondered what she would have done if anyone other than me had answered the phone. I couldn't see her asking Mum that question.

I told her that he wasn't.

'Has he not come home yet?' It was like she was begging me to say that he had.

'I'm sorry, no.' I apologised because I knew that I wasn't telling her what she wanted to hear.

'I'm really going to have to tell them, aren't I?'

I didn't think it was a real question so I didn't offer an answer. I just offered another apology. When I put the phone down I realised that Mum was standing behind me. I apologised to her too.

ROBERT

I didn't have a destination in mind when I set off. You know, it wasn't like I was thinking *I'm going to go to such and such,* I was just driving. Thank God traffic was light on the motorway because my mind wasn't exactly on the road ahead.

Despite what you might think about me being a selfish prick it's not like I didn't give a second thought to those I'd left behind and what I'd left them with. But, do you know what? There's no point lying about it; I might as well tell you exactly what I was thinking as I drove. I was wondering how far I could get before anyone realised I was gone. Michelle wouldn't be home until after five, so she'd be in the dark for a while, and Tom wouldn't get his note till just before then. Mum, on the other hand, would be home about three unless she went shopping. So who knew? I certainly didn't. I didn't have a bloody clue about anything.

I wondered how they'd react when they found their notes. I thought that Mum and Michelle would be upset but Tom probably wouldn't give a toss. Would it have been easier for them if I'd told them in person rather than in a note? For them maybe, but not for me. Mum might have been OK, because I was always going to leave home sometime, but I doubted that Michelle hearing the words come out of my mouth would have softened the blow for her. And it would be a blow – I knew it would – but, the truth is, I just didn't care enough to do things differently. I had a life to live and it didn't involve being a father.

Don't you think I knew that I was being selfish?

Anyway, I'm not going to apologise for what I was doing. I'd spent half the night worrying about it, I'd made a decision, and I was sticking to it. Simple as.

But that didn't stop me thinking about it as I drove down the A1 going God knows where.

I misjudged pulling out in front of a white van at one point and nearly got wiped out. Only the sound of someone leaning on the horn made me aware of them. I quickly pulled back into the left-hand lane and, as the van passed, saw the driver waving in my direction. You didn't need to be a lip reader to work out that he was effing and blinding at me. He even gave me the middle finger for good measure just in case I hadn't got the message. I put my hand up in a pathetic attempt to apologise for nearly killing us both.

Not long after that I noticed the brake lights of the vehicles ahead of me lighting up as the traffic slowed and eventually stopped. I hadn't noticed warning signs for road works so all I could assume was that there had been an accident. A girl driving a green Mini that was stopped in the lane beside me mouthed the words, 'What's going on?' and I shrugged my shoulders. She smiled at me and on any other day I'd have been chuffed, but that day it was the last thing I wanted so I turned away and stared straight ahead.

Five or six minutes later I saw the blue lights of the

emergency vehicles coming up behind me. The daylight was fading so as the police car and ambulance came down the hard shoulder their lights brightened up the inside of my car.

The contrast wasn't lost on me. I'd thought I was having a bad day, but apparently there was someone having a much worse one than me. Mum always said 'It doesn't matter what happens there's always someone worse off than you are,' but, as I told her every time she quoted those words of wisdom, that doesn't solve your problems does it? I was sorry for whoever was involved in whatever the police and ambulance were attending, and I hoped they'd be OK, but their having problems didn't lessen mine.

We'd been there for a while before I even looked at the clock and we still hadn't moved a good ten minutes after that. We were just there, stationary, for what felt like ages and I spent the time wondering how the hell I'd let myself get caught up in this mess.

With the light almost gone, I made a mental note to put the headlights on if we ever started moving again. Eventually we did start to move, and not before time: patience has never been my strong suit and sitting there not going anywhere was doing my head in. We inched along, which would normally have irritated the life out of me, but on that occasion it was fine because controlling the car's movement using the clutch gave me something else to think about.

As I came to a bend in the road all I could see was traffic nose to tail. I looked at the petrol gauge and hoped that I wouldn't run out of fuel. It showed just under a quarter of a tank and I didn't relish the idea of paying motorway prices. And then I saw the sign for the next exit. It was a mile away and I finally knew where I was going.

I crawled forwards towards the slip road, along with everyone else, and when I was within half a mile of it I thought *sod it,* checked my mirrors and moved onto the hard shoulder. I was pretty sure that the police had more important things to worry about than me using the emergency lane, so I thought I'd get away with it. I had to suffer the glares of some of my fellow drivers but it was probably jealousy rather than anger and as I looked in the rear-view mirror I saw others follow where I had led.

At the top of the slip road I took the third exit at the roundabout and headed for the coast.

It was dark by the time I got there, but I knew that if it had still been light I would have been able to see the sea from where I was. We used to go there every July for two weeks and that spot at the top of the hill was where me and Tom would compete to be the first to see the sea.

I felt better than I had all day.

The good thing about a seaside town is that there are plenty of hotels and B&Bs to choose from, but it was only after I'd walked up and down the street that we had always stayed on that I realised that it was the off season and every window had a 'Closed' sign in it. Undeterred, I got back in the car and drove around the bay to what Tom and I had always thought of as the lively part of town.

It wasn't lively that night though, which wasn't surprising I suppose. There were a few people walking along the sea front on their way to somewhere but I could probably have counted them all on the fingers of one hand.

I parked the car, got out and leaned against the railings to listen to the sea. I could hear the waves lapping on the beach, though they sounded a distance away so I guessed that the tide was out. I thought about going onto the beach and walking. Not walking along the beach... walking into the sea. Would I have the bottle to keep going while the water came up around my ankles? My knees? Would I carry on walking, or would instinct take over and force me to swim? I'm a good swimmer, so what if I kept swimming? Just kept going further and further out into whatever sea it was – the North I think. Surely there'd come a point where I couldn't swim any more and the sea would take me.

I thought about the car parked there: off season or not, I was sure that someone would notice it. I hadn't looked, but there was more than likely a parking fee I should have paid. Would some eagle-eyed traffic warden put a ticket on it and then report it to the police when it hadn't moved for a while? I imagined them checking the registration and turning up at my home address asking if I was there and had my car been stolen. My parents would come looking for me, I was sure of that. Well, Mum would anyway; she'd spend the rest of her life searching for me in this town, or at least until they found my body. If they found my body...

I stopped that train of thought right there because A: I

39

didn't want Mum walking around this town for the next thirty years like some deranged old woman from a Brontë novel and B: I didn't want to die. The reason that I hadn't wanted to be tied down to Michelle and some kid that she might be having was because I had too much living left to do.

I tried to focus. I needed a place to stay but if push came to shove, I could sleep in the car. I also needed to eat. I hadn't had anything since the night before and I was starving.

I ate fish and chips sitting on a bench on the sea front. My dad had bought us fish and chips from that particular chip shop many times over the years but we'd always sat inside, eating the food off plates with knives and forks, and accompanied by bread and butter and cups of tea. That night I sat in the dark eating out of the paper with my fingers. The chips tasted as good as they always had, maybe even a bit better.

It was freezing by then and the only person to pass me was a man walking his dog. The dog made a bee-line for me and the man pulled him away saying, 'Come away, Bob.'

For a split second I thought he was talking to me. I know that technically my dad was the 'Bob' of the family, but it threw me just the same. I've never understood why people give dogs human names.

Anyway, Bob was dragged off still looking towards me and sniffing the chips for as long as he could. Well he could bugger off because he wasn't getting any. I was fully aware of the situation I was in and what it meant financially. I had a few quid in my pocket and a bank card that gave me access to some more but, now that I was out of work, I was going to have to make it last. These fish and chips might have to fill me for a few days, so Bob was getting nowt.

I threw the paper into a dustbin but only after I'd wiped every morsel up with my fingers and licked them clean: salt, vinegar, grease – the lot.

I walked around for a bit to clear my head. I thought about going for a pint in the pub at the end of the sea front but then thought I'd probably pay twice what I would at home – and one wouldn't be enough: there was a good chance that if I went in I wouldn't stop drinking until my pockets were empty and that wasn't a luxury that I could afford.

I didn't recognise myself; I'd become sensible overnight.

I walked back to the car and got in. I sat looking into the darkness for God knows how long until, gradually, the few places that were open started to close and soon there was almost total darkness. Even the streetlights had dimmed.

I'd barely slept the night before and driven for hours so I was completely shattered. I couldn't bring myself to move another inch until I had slept, so I laid my head back against the seat rest and closed my eyes.

I didn't get to sleep for a long time. When I woke, it was to the sound of seagulls. A few seconds later I realised that I had a crick in my neck. I'd sort of squirmed around in the seat and was almost in a foetal position with my right hip wedged against the steering wheel. Once I'd slowly straightened myself out I looked at the time. It was almost seven o'clock. It was still dark but there was a faint hint of sunrise way off on the horizon.

My neck creaked as I moved my head from side to side and though I didn't feel particularly rested I knew that I'd at least be able to put one foot in front of the other now.

Not that I did, not straight away anyway. What would be the point? It was still dark and nowhere would be open.

I wondered how Michelle had slept. I wondered if she was all right and if she'd told her parents about the baby yet. That's if there was a baby, of course.

You're probably thinking that I should have made sure of that before I threw everything away – and maybe you're right – but even if she wasn't pregnant and was just using it as a scam to get me to the altar it was still something I wanted no part of. Call me selfish if you like, and there'll be plenty that do, but I just didn't want anything that Michelle was part of.

So there I was in a seaside town, in February, with no home, no job and very little money. *Welcome to your new life, my son.*

I went for another walk just to get my kinks straightened out and then, a bit later on, I drove up into the town. I'd established the night before that I wasn't going to walk into the sea and disappear, so I went in search of the things I needed. First on the list was a strong cup of tea.

42

TOM

Mum didn't go to work the day after Robert left.

'What would be the point?' she said. 'I wouldn't be able to concentrate on anything. And anyway, I want to be here when…' She didn't finish the sentence, she didn't have to.

'When what?' Dad asked as he grabbed his coat from the back of the kitchen door. He put it on and pulled at the collar to straighten it, never taking his eyes off Mum. He was waiting for an answer but she didn't have one. She couldn't even look at him.

I'd been sitting at the table with her, eating toast that neither of us wanted, before Dad came in, then she got up and cleared the dishes away. Anything to avoid looking at him. The thing about Dad, though, is that he can be a bit like a dog with a bone and he wasn't going to let it go.

'Don't be expecting him to come home,' he said, 'because you're wasting your time.'

'He might ring.' She lowered the dishes into the sink and started to wash them. She'd obviously spent most of her sleepless night crying and I'd felt sorry enough for her when we were sitting at the table, but it was even worse watching her at the sink with her back to me. Her shoulders were stooped and she had a defeated air about her.

Dad must have felt her pain too because he kissed her cheek tenderly as he grabbed his packed lunch from where she'd left it on the work bench. He mouthed the words, 'He won't,' to me and shouted, 'See you later love,' to Mum on his way to the front door.

'Did you get any sleep?' I asked her as she leant against the sink drying her hands on a tea towel.

'A little,' she said, turning to face me. I didn't believe her.

'You were up early,' I continued after a couple of seconds, and immediately wished I hadn't because her face looked even more pained.

'I'm sorry,' she sighed. 'I didn't mean to wake you.'

'You didn't,' I said quickly. 'I didn't get much sleep either.'

She forced a smile onto her face before looking off to the side.

'Are you all right, Mum?' I asked. I knew it was a stupid question but I didn't know what else to say.

'Why?'

Even though she was facing the wall, I heard the question. Not that I knew how to answer her. Was she asking me why I was asking her if she was all right?

After a few seconds she turned to look at me and asked, 'Why?' again.

This time I knew what she meant. I could tell by the look in her eyes. I answered the only way I could.

'I don't know.'

'Did he not say *anything* to you, Tom?' she pleaded. 'Did he not say where he was going?'

I took in a slow deep breath and let it out the same way. 'The first I knew about it was yesterday,' I told her, 'when

I found you holding that letter in your hands.'

'But you talked.' She sounded desperate, but I had no hope to give her.

'No, we didn't,' I admitted. 'Not recently anyway. Not about anything that mattered.'

'I don't understand,' she said, as she picked up a plate from the drainer and went through the motions of drying it. 'How could he do this to me?'

'How could he do it to Michelle?' I said, as I got up from the table and prepared to leave. I felt an anger rising in my stomach and the chair scraped on the floor as I pushed it in. 'How could he do it to his baby?'

She looked embarrassed. 'I know, I know,' she said. 'I feel for the girl, I really do.'

'You should,' I said as I leaned on the back of the chair, 'because it doesn't get any lower than this.' I might as well have slapped her in the face because she visibly flinched when I said that. 'I'm sorry,' I said, 'but I can't feel any sympathy for him.'

'He's scared, that's all,' she said defensively.

'And Michelle's terrified,' I said defiantly, 'but she can't just run away from it.'

I'd turned to leave and was almost through the door when Mum asked, 'What's she going to do?'

I pretended not to hear. I just couldn't talk about it any more. We weren't going to agree about what Robert had done or his reasons for doing it and I didn't want to argue.

I left her alone to wait for a phone call that wouldn't come.

45

'Have you seen him?' Michelle didn't ask it like she was expecting me to say yes.

Just as well.

'So, what are you doing here?'

I shrugged my shoulders and felt a bit foolish as I said, 'I don't know.'

'Do you want to come in?' She stepped back like she was inviting me in and I looked at her, not knowing what I should do. I really didn't know why I was there, so I definitely wasn't sure if I should go in. I think she got bored of waiting for an answer because she turned away and walked back into the house leaving the door open for me to do what I liked.

I went in.

She'd stopped outside the room that I'd seen her parents in a few days earlier. She used her head to gesture towards it. I met her eyes briefly as I passed through the doorway – narrow eyes, like she was trying to weigh something up.

She indicated the chair that I should sit in and once again I did what I was told. She lowered herself into the one opposite. She looked intently down at her hands and her fingers plucked at each other. When she looked up again, I turned away as quickly as I could. I didn't want her to think I'd been staring at her.

She took a deep breath. 'I thought you'd come to tell me that he was back,' she said.

I couldn't imagine why she would think that, but my guess was that she was living more in hope than expectation. 'Sorry,' I said, with an apologetic shrug.

She was blinking her eyes quickly, obviously trying to stop herself from crying. 'He's not coming back, is he.' She said it as a statement of fact rather than a question.

I answered her as honestly as I could.

'I don't think so.'

'*Why?*' Michelle lost another battle with the tears and I saw one trickling down each cheek. I asked myself how many tears it was possible for one person to cry. She looked at a spot over my shoulder and seemed lost in her own world. 'Why would he do this to me? Why would he do it to our baby? How could he do it?' She was asking the questions without waiting for an answer and I was thankful for that. 'I thought he loved me,' she said as she wiped the tears away from her cheeks and I couldn't fail to see how sad her eyes looked. 'I guess I was wrong.' She pulled a tissue from the sleeve of her cardigan and blew her nose. Then, taking me completely by surprise, she asked, 'How's your mum?'

'She's OK,' I lied.

'Really?' I could tell she didn't believe me.

'No,' I admitted, 'not really. She hasn't been back to work since he left and there's no food in the house.'

Michelle looked puzzled, so I explained.

'She's scared that if she leaves the house Robert'll ring while she's out.'

Michelle nodded her head slowly. 'I'm a bit like that myself.'

'Don't be,' I told her. 'He's not worth it.'

47

She looked at the floor and caught her lower lip between her teeth. I almost asked her what she was thinking, but decided against it. You didn't need to be a genius to know her thoughts were on Robert. She sat like that for a full minute. It turned out that she was trying to decide whether she should tell me something or not. She decided to spill the beans.

'Mum wants me to get rid of it,' she said. 'She says that I should get something from the hospital that'll make it go away.' She finally lifted her eyes and looked at me as though she wanted to see my reaction.

'Will you?' I kept my voice as flat as I could because I didn't want her to think that I was judging her.

She pushed herself into an upright position and slowly said, 'I'm a nurse Tom. It's my job to save lives not take them.' She paused long enough to take in and let out a deep breath. 'Besides, I want this baby.'

I didn't need to ask her why. Even I could work out that if she had his baby she would have a little piece of Robert too.

I could hear the raised voices before I even got to the door. It was unusual for my parents to argue, but they'd done quite a lot of it in the week since Robert had left. The whole street could probably hear them that day, though.

I heard Mum shout, 'But we don't know where he *is*, Bob.'

'You want to thank God that we don't know where he is,' Dad shouted back, 'because if we did, I'd kill him. And then we really would need the coppers!' He came out of the room so fast that he nearly bumped into me and there was a look in his eyes I had never seen before. He wasn't just angry; he'd left angry way behind.

He snatched his coat from where it was hanging in the hallway and disappeared out of the door. I looked at the door for a few seconds wondering if I should go after him but, in the end, I decided to go and see if Mum was all right. I popped my head slowly around the door and saw that she was looking out of the window. I stood behind her and we both watched my dad as he sat in the car.

His back was ramrod stiff and he was looking straight ahead. His hands were on the steering wheel and even from that distance I thought I could see the whites of his knuckles.

Mum leaned into me and I put my arm around her shoulder.

'He's hurting too,' I told her.

'Is he?' she asked.

Five minutes later I'd managed to get Mum into a chair and told her to stay where she was. She seemed to be in a sort of a daze so I didn't think she'd go very far. I went outside, opened the door to my father's car and climbed in.

We sat in silence for what felt like ages but was probably only a couple of minutes, if that.

'Your mum wants to call the police,' he said eventually.

'I know,' I said.

'Do you think we should?'

Out of the corner of my eye I saw him turn to look at

me.

I turned to face him and said, 'No.'

'There's no point, Mum,' I said. Dad and I had come back into the house together and found Mum still sitting where I'd left her. I knelt beside her and stroked her hand while Dad stood behind me. 'Robert's not missing, Mum. He hasn't gone missing – he chose to leave.'

ROBERT

I drove up into the town and parked the car in a side street.

When we'd been there on holiday, we hadn't spent a lot of time in the town centre, but there was something familiar about it that brought me a bit of comfort. I followed the smell of bacon to a café and went inside. Tempted as I was by the Full English – five items for less than four quid – I ordered a cup of tea and left it at that. I'd checked my wallet and realised that I had less than twenty on me and I wanted to hang onto that for as long as I could. I'd need to find a bank to check exactly how much I was worth. I didn't anticipate it being a lot.

There were a couple of blokes eating breakfast at one of the tables but other than that it was just me and the woman behind the counter. I'd thought that she looked about my age when I first saw her, but closer inspection added a good fifteen or twenty years to that.

'Can I get you anything else, love?' she asked as she put the mug of tea in front of me.

'No, ta,' I said and I took a long slug of the drink she had brought. I swear to God that nothing in my life had tasted as good as the tea did that morning.

I nursed the mug for as long as I could because, not long after I'd gone into the café, it had started to pelt it down with rain. The woman behind the counter didn't seem to mind because once the two blokes had finished their breakfast it was just the two of us and I think she was glad of the company. She told me her name was Tanya.

I was probably in there for an hour or so before the rain stopped, though it was still grey overhead and looked like it would be back again before too long. I took my chance to head out for a look around the town.

The shops that sold buckets and spades and holiday souvenirs were still boarded up. It'd be a good six or eight weeks before the tourists started to arrive in numbers. I thought the place looked a bit sad, but that suited my mood to a tee. I didn't want to be there; I'd far rather have been changing a gear box or stripping an engine that morning. One thing I had noticed was that I hadn't passed a garage, so I was a bit concerned about my job prospects. Mind, I couldn't see Bill, my old boss, giving me a good reference, so I was probably buggered anyway as far as being a mechanic was concerned. I thought I might need to consider a change in career.

A trip to the bank told me that I had £201.96 in my account. I thought about getting some more cash out, but I didn't want to be tempted to spend it.

I had another bag of chips at tea-time and slept in the car again that night.

I went to the café again the following morning. Well, I didn't have anywhere else to go, so why not? The place was clean, it was handy and Tanya knew her way around a teapot. She was clearing a table when I went in, balancing plates along the length of her arm.

'Morning, Rob,' she said with a smile.

My stomach did a funny little turn thing when she called me Rob. I'd told her that my name was Robert. She had shortened it herself. Bob was my dad, Bobby was the bloke that Michelle loved, and Robert was the shit that had walked out on her. Nobody had ever called me Rob before. I liked it. Rob was someone different. Rob was someone new. Rob could be anyone he wanted to be.

'You look like crap,' Tanya said as she put a mug of tea on the table in front of me.

I knew she was right but I tried to make a joke of it and said something like, 'Oh, cheers for that Tanya.'

She looked at the only other person in the café, checking that he was OK for coffee, and when she was satisfied that he was, she sat down on the chair opposite mine. She rested her elbows on the table and leaned in towards me.

'Where'd you sleep last night?' she asked. 'On a park bench?'

I tried to ignore her question by taking a mouthful of the tea, which was boiling. I thought a blister or two would be worth it if she changed the subject. She didn't, she just looked at me with one eyebrow raised.

'Of course I didn't.' I tried to force a laugh.

I could tell from her face that I hadn't convinced her.

'What are you running away from, Rob?' she asked.

Her question took me by surprise and I spluttered out something like, 'Nothing! What would make you ask that?'

She shrugged her shoulders and said, 'Call it a wild

guess.' She turned her head at the sound of cutlery being set on a plate. 'You finished, Charlie?' she asked, pushing herself out of the chair and giving me one last look over her shoulder as she walked away. 'Can I get you anything else?' she asked as she picked up Charlie's empty plate and empty mug. He smiled, shook his head, and handed her some money. He nodded at me on his way out.

'You had any breakfast? Tanya shouted from behind the counter. I thought about lying and saying that I had but, in the end, I told the truth. 'Thought not,' she said. She appeared at my shoulder, 'Here,' she said, putting a small plate in front of me.

I looked at the bacon sandwich on the plate and asked, 'What's this for?'

'What do you think?' she put her hands on her hips and her head on one side. 'It's so you can line your shoes and save your insoles.'

'No,' I actually did laugh that time because I thought it was funny. 'What... what I mean is... why are you giving it to me?'

'Because I'm soft in the head,' she smiled and walked away.

I can still remember how I felt that day. I sat looking at the sandwich with a smile on my face marvelling at the kindness of someone I barely knew.

God that bacon sarnie was good. Thick buttered white bread with five or six pieces of bacon. I was starving and it barely touched the sides as I wolfed it down. I emptied the dregs of my tea and took the mug and the plate back to the counter. I went to my pocket to get my wallet out but Tanya waved it away.

'Call it my treat.'

I made a pretence of insisting that I would pay but to be honest I couldn't afford to look a gift horse in the mouth so I accepted with a smile.

'Thanks, Tanya,' I said. 'See you.'

I was walking to the door when I heard her call my name.

'Rob,' she said, 'I finish at twelve. You could meet me if you like.'

I did like. Of course I did. But later, as I leaned against the wall waiting for Tanya to come out, I asked myself what the hell I was doing.

'Where's your car?' she asked before she'd even closed the café door behind her. I asked her how she knew I had a car and she said, 'Well you said that you hadn't slept on a park bench so...' she didn't finish her sentence.

Ten minutes later we were sitting in the kitchen of Tanya's house. I sat at the table and watched her make sandwiches.

'Cheese all right?' she asked, and I said that it was. I think she asked the question out of politeness more than anything else because the sandwich had practically already been made before I answered. She brought the food to the table and sat opposite me.

'So,' she said, as she prepared to take a bite from the sandwich in her hand, 'are you going to tell me the truth this time?'

'About what?' I'd already started eating so my words were a bit muffled, but I was sure she'd got the gist of it.

She swallowed the bite that she'd taken and put the sandwich down on her plate. She dabbed the corner of her mouth and I was surprised by how alluring I found that.

'I asked you a question earlier,' she said, 'and I don't think that you told me the truth.' We looked at each other and then she asked, 'What are you running away from?'

She sat back in the chair but she held my gaze. 'Tell me to mind my own business if you want, just don't tell me that I'm wrong.'

During the next hour I told Tanya about Michelle, the baby, and the life that I wasn't ready for – the life I didn't want.

'How did she take it?' Tanya asked when I'd finally talked myself out.

I was more embarrassed than I'd thought I would be when I admitted that I didn't know because I hadn't spoken to her.

Tanya set her head to one side, you know, the way people do when they're asking a question without words.

'I wrote her a note,' I said reluctantly. I don't know why I had felt the need to tell Tanya the truth, why I hadn't just said something like Michelle had cried her eyes out and begged me to stay.

She nodded her head slowly, still not taking her eyes off me.

I don't remember the exact details of what we said, or

when we said it, but I can tell you that she didn't judge me. She didn't even offer an opinion, as far as I can remember.

Half an hour later we were lying together in her bed.

It hadn't been my intention to end up there, and I don't think it'd been Tanya's either. It just happened.

I never had to sleep in the car again.

TOM

Robert had been gone for about a week before Mum even asked how Michelle was.

I didn't really know how to answer that one because I wasn't sure if she would want the truth. Would she want to know that Michelle still hadn't been back to work? Would she want to know that she had cried almost every waking hour since Robert had left? Would she want to know that Michelle threw up every time she as much as smelled an orange?

In the end I said, 'She's OK.'

It was two weeks after Robert left that Michelle finally went back to work and two weeks after that she finally stopped crying for him.

'What's the point?' she said to me one day. 'He's not coming back...' she paused a second or two before she added, 'is he?'

I knew what she wanted me to say but I still couldn't bring myself to do it. I couldn't give her false hope.

'No,' I said, 'he's not.'

I looked at her and saw sadness all over her face. I felt like I had grabbed her last piece of hope away from her.

'Anyway,' I said, 'even if he came back, why would you want him? Why would you want him after what he's done to you?'

She faced me but her eyes flitted from side to side. 'I don't think I would,' she said finally, 'but I think I'd like to have the chance to hurt him as much as he's hurt me.'

I remember smiling at her and saying, 'Good for you.' I smiled because it seemed that the scales had fallen from her eyes and she was finally seeing my brother for the knobhead that he was. However, although she was making all the right noises, I wasn't convinced that she actually meant what she was saying. It was how she *wanted* to feel, I think, I just didn't believe she was *actually* feeling it yet.

I wanted to put my arms around her and tell her that everything would be all right but I didn't think she'd feel that yet either.

'Thank you for everything, Tom,' she said, and I told her that she was welcome.

A day or two after she'd asked me if Robert was coming back we were sitting on opposite ends of the sofa in the living room of her parents' house. I looked up when something caught my eye and saw that her mother had stopped on her way to wherever she was going. She moved along when Michelle glanced up at her and the pair shared a *look*. Michelle turned back to me and said, 'The thing is, Tom,' she spoke slowly like she was struggling to find the right words, 'I'll be all right,' she paused a second or two before she added, 'now.'

I was confused. Come on, I'm a bloke, I don't do subtlety.

'I don't know what you mean,' I said.

'I mean,' she gave herself a bit of thinking time, 'I mean that you have done everything that you need to do, more than I would ever have expected of you and now it's time to get on with your own life.'

It took a few seconds before the penny finally dropped. 'Is that what you think I've been doing,' I asked, 'coming here out of some sort of *duty*?' I did that quotation mark thing in the air. 'Do you think that I've been coming here to clear up Robert's mess?'

'Why else?' she asked.

I had asked myself the same question more than once and before I knew it I was saying, 'At first, I came here because, like you said, I was clearing up my brother's mess – and let's be honest, it's a hell of a mess.'

Michelle surprised both of us by laughing at that, which was a relief because God knows why I had said it. We looked at each other for a few seconds.

'I will be all right,' she said again quietly, without much conviction.

'I know you will,' I said. I hadn't planned on then saying, 'So would it be all right if I carried on coming to see you just because I wanted to?' But I did.

'That would be lovely,' she said quickly, and I don't know if she realised that she took a sly look towards where her mother had been standing.

Before I left, we agreed to meet a couple of nights later. I said that I would meet her from work. I've got to be honest and tell you that as I walked home that night I asked myself why I'd said what I had, why I'd come on to my brother's ex. Was it weird? I decided it wasn't really, because I wasn't thinking of her in those terms. At the end of the day, she was Michelle: a girl that I knew from school. A girl that I'd liked and had asked out. What was wrong with that?

I'd no sooner rationalised the thought in my head than another problem popped in. Why had she agreed to go out with me? Was it because I reminded her of Robert? I'm not saying that we're almost identical twins or anything but there is a similarity between us – in looks at least, I would never have done what he had.

I'm going to be honest and tell you that I spent a fair bit of time wondering about her motives but, in the end, I decided to go with the flow. What was the worst that could happen?

So I met her from work as promised a couple of nights later and we went to a pizza place to get something to eat. It was a bit awkward at first... well, you know what it's like when you go on a first date. We were shown to a table and ordered a couple of drinks while we checked out the menu – it wasn't much of a menu. We decided to share a pizza, pepperoni probably as it's Michelle's favourite, and she ordered a salad on the side.

'How've you been?' I asked once the waitress had walked away. It was something to say.

'OK, thanks,' she said.

Well, that was the end of that conversation. It was ridiculous how nervous I felt. I'd known her for years and it wasn't even as if this was the first time we'd eaten together. She'd come to our house for tea, or Sunday lunch, loads of times when she was with Robert.

But she wasn't with Robert now was she? She was with me and that made this time different. I wondered if she was feeling as nervous as I was. I thought she probably was.

'Do your mum and dad know you're here?' she asked.

'No,' I said. 'Do yours?'

'God, no,' she said, and we both laughed.

The food arrived before the laughter faded to an awkward silence, and I thanked God for thin crusts and pizza ovens – in my experience, pizza makes any situation easier.

The waitress put the large pizza in the middle of the table and two small plates in front of us. She put the salad at Michelle's elbow. The pizza slicer provided wasn't really big enough for the slices of pizza but I managed to manoeuvre a piece onto each of our plates without dropping anything. I was pleased to see that Michelle picked hers up to eat it. I don't understand why anyone would eat pizza with a knife and fork and I was glad to see that she wasn't one of them. That could have been a deal breaker.

'What do you think they'd say?' she asked just before she put the pointy end of the pizza into her mouth.

'Can't imagine my mum would be very happy,' I said, though I thought I might be underestimating her reaction.

She threw her head back and laughed out loud and I couldn't help smiling at her. 'Well my mum would go doolally,' she said.

We ate in silence for a couple of minutes before I asked, 'Where have you told her you are?'

'Having pizza with a friend.' She popped the last bite in her mouth, chewed it, swallowed it and shrugged her shoulders. 'Well I'm not lying, am I?'

I'm grinning just thinking about when she said that. She made it sound like we were taking part in some sort of conspiracy. In a way I suppose we were. Anyway, I served her another slice and she licked her fingers before picking it up.

'Does it bother you?' she asked as she took another bite. I was pleased to see that she'd clearly got her appetite back.

'Does what bother me?' I asked. I knew fine well what she was talking about but I let her spell it out for me anyway.

'Me not telling them that you were the friend I was meeting?'

'No,' I said, 'Why should it? I didn't tell my parents either…'

I took her home of course but as we walked along, mainly in companionable silence, I wondered how far I should take her. She hadn't told her parents that she was meeting me so I guessed that she wouldn't want them seeing us together.

She must have been thinking along the same lines because when we got to the end of the street she asked, 'Do you want to leave me here?'

I looked along the street and was surprised to see that it

was only dimly lit. A few of the lights were out and clearly the council hadn't got around to fixing them yet. Michelle was looking towards her house which was still a few hundred yards away.

'I could take you further if you like.' I said. I didn't want to force anything but I didn't like the idea of leaving her. If the street lights had been working I could have watched her to her door but... well, they weren't, and I just didn't like the idea of leaving her.

'Oh, do you know what,' she said as she linked her arm through mine, 'sod it. Come on, I'm not ashamed of being out with you.'

I wasn't ashamed either so I walked her all the way to the front door.

When her key was in the lock she turned to me and said, 'I've had a lovely time Tom. I'm pleased that you suggested it.'

'I had a good time too,' I said, which was the truth.

She opened the door and prepared to go inside. 'Maybe we could do it again,' she said and as she spoke she gave me that flirty little look that girls do. You know the one, where their head is lowered a bit and they sort lift their eyes up to you. That was when I first dared to hope that Michelle might be feeling the same way I was.

I told her that I'd like that. And I could hardly wait.

'I didn't hear you come in last night,' Mum said over breakfast the following morning.

'Good,' I started buttering a piece of toast, 'I must be

getting better at creeping in.' I made a joke of it, but I really was glad that she hadn't heard me because it meant that she must be sleeping again and that was a good sign. During those first few nights after Robert had left I'd heard her tossing and turning in the bedroom next to mine before going downstairs in the wee small hours. I looked at her as she pottered around the kitchen and noticed that she actually looked a little better.

I took another piece of toast and buttered it while I decided whether I should tell them where I had been the evening before. Well not so much where I'd been, but rather who I was with. I remembered Michelle saying 'sod it' just before she put her arm through mine, and I decided to take the same attitude.

'Me and Michelle went out for a pizza,' I said casually.

Mum was half way through swallowing her tea when she started to choke and cough. She recovered enough to splutter out the words, 'Robert's Michelle?'

'Well,' I said, leaning back in my chair, 'I think she stopped being Robert's Michelle when he walked out on her, don't you?'

She didn't answer me. She just gave me a look that said she couldn't believe what she was hearing.

'Where did you take her?' she asked as she started to noisily clear away the dishes.

'I didn't *take* her anywhere,' I said, making sure that I emphasised the word. '*We*' – I emphasised that word too – 'went for a pizza.'

Up to that point my father hadn't said a word as we ate

breakfast but then he asked, 'How's she keeping?' without looking up from his paper. I don't think he was reading it as much as using it to hide behind.

'She's all right,' I told him. 'She still gets sick when she smells oranges, but apart from that she seems fine.'

We went to the pictures the following week. I can't remember what we were going to see but I remember that we had to queue up to get in. As we waited I couldn't help noticing that Michelle seemed a bit... I'm still not sure what it was exactly, but I just sensed that there was something wrong with her. I asked her what it was.

'Nothing,' she said but I could tell she was lying: you know, she said it in that way that people have of saying *nothing* when they really mean *something*. She paused and looked straight ahead and I had a bad feeling in the pit of my stomach.

'This might not be such a good idea,' she said.

I was quickly trying to come up with a cool response to being binned off when she said, 'I mean, look at this queue. We're not going to get in.'

I can't tell you how relieved I was when I realised she was talking about the film.

'Anyway,' she looked at me, 'I think we need to talk.' I wondered if my relief had been premature.

We stepped out of the queue and everyone behind us shuffled forward.

There was hardly a soul in the Black Horse but that didn't stop Michelle from finding the table furthest from the bar and the few people that were there. She sat down while I went to get the drinks. As I stood waiting to be served my mind fizzed with thoughts of what Michelle wanted to talk about. Maybe she was going to give me the elbow after all. *Oh well,* I thought, *won't be the first time.*

I put Michelle's drink on the table and sat on the stool opposite her. I took a swig of my pint and put it carefully onto the beer mat.

'Are you going to tell me what's wrong?' I asked.

'Who says that there's anything wrong?' she asked without taking her eyes off her drink. She waited a moment or two before asking 'What's happening here, Tom?'

'What do you mean?' I asked, though I was thinking *here it comes.*

She took a sip of her drink, taking much longer than was necessary, allowing herself time to think. 'Mum came into my room tonight as I was getting ready,' she said, 'and asked me what I was doing.' She paused to take a couple of deep breaths. 'I told her not to worry but she said how could she not?' She finally looked up at me.

'What's she worried about?' I asked.

'*Us.*' She made it sound like I'd asked a stupid question.

'And why's she worried about us?' I tried to sound casual.

'She's worried,' Michelle said slowly, like she was trying to explain something to a small child, 'because you're Robert's brother.'

'You shouldn't hold that against me,' I said.

'I don't,' she whispered.

I took a gulp of beer and, as I set the glass down, I told her, 'If it's any consolation my mother's not wild about me seeing you either.'

She gave a little laugh. 'I shouldn't imagine she is.'

I gave it a couple of seconds before I told her, 'She calls you "Robert's Michelle".'

'I am not Robert's anything,' she said defiantly, squinting her eyes to emphasise the point.

I smiled at her and said, 'I know you're not.' I reached across the table and put my hand on her arm. 'And while I can't deny that I am Robert's brother, I am *not him*. You know that.'

She touched my hand. 'I know you're not, Tom. And that's what scares me.'

'You have nothing to be scared of, Michelle,' I assured her.

We sat for a few seconds as she stroked the hand that I had rested on her arm. Then she took a deep breath and asked, 'What do you want from me, Tom?'

I didn't answer straight away, and maybe she thought that I hadn't heard her, so she asked the question again. 'What do you want from me, Tom?'

'I don't want anything,' the words came out carefully as I tried to work out the right way to say it, 'at least, not anything from you that you don't want to give me.'

Her lips were trembling and I thought that she was going to cry. She didn't, but she did admit, 'I am so scared Tom.'

'You have *nothing* to be scared of,' I told her again.

'He hurt me so much,' she sniffed and swallowed hard.

'But I'm not him,' I squeezed her arm to emphasise the point.

'I know you're not,' she said quietly. 'And that's what scares me the most.'

I think I understood where she was coming from – I'd probably have felt the same if I'd been in her place.

'What are you doing with me, Tom?' she asked.

I couldn't help myself and said flippantly, 'Having a drink.'

'Please, Tom,' she said seriously. 'There's something I have to understand.'

'What do you want to know?' I asked.

'Be honest with me,' she said and then quickly apologised for having said that. She took another deep breath and asked, 'What do you want from this relationship?'

That was a tricky one because I'd said that I would answer honestly and the honest answer was that I didn't know. I chose my words carefully.

'At first, I just wanted friendship,' I said, 'you and I were friends long ago and I want us to be friends a long time from now.' I was stretching the truth a bit about us being friends long ago, but she used to smile at me from time to time so that had made us friends in my book. I took a long slug on my beer for Dutch courage. 'But I'd be lying to you, Michelle,' I said, 'if I said that I didn't want more than that now.'

I knew that she was looking at me but I didn't take my

eyes off my pint. 'I don't know how far we can go with this, but I want us to take it as far as we can.' As soon as the words were out of my mouth I took another gulp of beer.

'You make it sound so simple,' Michelle said.

I shrugged my shoulders and told her, 'It'll be as easy or as hard as it will be and we'll deal with it.' I gave her a second or two to take in what I had said and then asked, 'What about you, Michelle? What do you want from this relationship?

'I...' she said the word slowly, stringing it out while she decided what it was that she wanted to say. She gave a little cough before she carried on, 'I like you Tom, I like you a lot and I've felt things in the past few weeks that I hadn't expected to feel again, at least not so soon. You make me laugh and you make me happy but then...'

'What?' I had to prompt her.

She took a deep breath and said, 'But then I remember the way things are.'

'And what way's that?' I knew what she meant but I needed to hear her say it.

'I'm pregnant,' she almost whispered it, but even so she looked around to check that no one had heard her.

'I know you are,' I said.

'And it's not *yours*.' She made it sound like she was telling me something that I didn't already know.

'I know that, too,' I said.

Then, she surprised the hell out of me by saying, 'I wish that it was.'

I surprised myself even more when I admitted, 'I wish it was too.'

That was the first night that I kissed her. There'd been pecks on the cheek before, and even one brief joining of lips, but that night I kissed her – really kissed her – and she kissed me back.

I can still see her face cupped between my hands as I tilted it towards me. I wanted to look at her so that I could see her eyes and know that this was what she really wanted. She looked as scared as I felt because we both knew that our relationship was moving to a new level.

Oh my God, she tasted so sweet!

As I walked home, I replayed the evening over and over in my head. In the space of a few hours I'd gone from thinking that she was going to finish with me to, well, being in a relationship with my brother's pregnant ex-girlfriend.

I asked myself two questions during that short walk. Firstly, would it really be as simple as I'd made it sound? And secondly, would my brother regret walking away from her?

I told myself that, firstly, life was only ever as complicated as you made it and, secondly, I didn't give a shit about what Robert regretted.

ROBERT

Tanya knew a bloke who knew a bloke who was looking for a barman so, by the end of the week, I was serving pints of beer in a pub that was off the beaten track but seemed to have loyal regulars.

'There's some odd bods,' Gloria, the landlord's wife, told me on my first day, 'but the regulars are a pub's lifeblood and we couldn't do without them.'

On that first afternoon I thought there were a few dodgy characters that they could do without, but I wasn't there to rock the boat so I kept my mouth shut.

Working behind a bar had never been part of the plan but I had to earn a living somehow. It wasn't much of a living – I earned a lot less than I had in the garage – but it was a wage and, at that point in my life, that was the important thing. I had a job and I had somewhere to live so I was doing all right.

'How was your first day?' Tanya asked when I got back to her flat. She didn't give me a chance to answer before she said, 'Don't worry, it'll get better. The place is buzzing during the season.'

Be that as it may, I hoped I wouldn't be there in the season to see it. Not as a member of staff anyway.

I thought about Michelle a fair bit during those first weeks. I know that on that first night, when she'd told me that she was pregnant, I'd hoped that there wasn't a baby but, in my heart, I knew there probably was. Hadn't I done a runner because I'd thought she was telling the truth?

Done a runner. I'd never have put me down as someone who would run, but, I had and there was no going back even if I'd wanted to. So, given that I thought Michelle was carrying my baby, of course I wondered how she was. I did think about ringing her but what would I say? Sorry I buggered off and left you to it? I didn't see that helping the situation. Anyway, I didn't want to give any clues as to where I was. I'm talking about the days before caller ID, so she couldn't have worked out where I was by using 1471, but maybe she could have overheard something – a seagull or some other sound that might give my location away. Look, I know it sounds stupid, and I'm embarrassed even to tell you, but I wasn't thinking straight.

Thank God there were no mobile phones back then. Can you imagine if I'd tried it now? I'd have had my mum on the phone every two minutes begging me to come home. I was fairly certain of that, you know: that my mother would have tried to persuade me to come home. I didn't think Dad would have been as keen, apart from to get me to do the decent thing by Michelle, and I reckoned our Tom wouldn't have cared either way, not really. By that time we weren't as close as we had been. Would Michelle have tried to get me to go home, too? Maybe at the beginning, but once she got her head around things she'd have worked out that she was better off without me. So, in the end, I decided to let sleeping dogs lie.

By the time that Easter was around the corner, I'd been working at The Brown Bull for about five or six weeks. The week before, Gloria had asked me how I was finding it.

'All right,' I'd told her. We were setting up the bar ready for opening time and we talked as we worked.

'Not what you're used to though, is it?'

I made a non-committal sort of noise because I didn't know what to say. I mean, she and her husband had given me a job and I was grateful for that. But she was right; it wasn't what I was used to. 'A change is as good as a rest,' I said.

She looked at me and said, 'You could be good at this if you gave it a chance. You have a good way with the customers.' She came towards me and handed over some beer mats to put out. 'I know it's not very exciting at the minute, we just sort of tick over at this time of year, but during the season it'll be busier.' Just before she walked away from me she said, 'Just give it a chance, Rob.'

I put the mats along the bar, taking a bit more care than necessary which gave me time to think about what Gloria had said. She was right when she said that I was good at the job. I know that sounds big-headed but the hardest part was learning how to pull a good pint and I'd picked that up pretty quickly. It wasn't working with cars but, to be honest, I didn't mind it. I enjoyed talking about football all day and Gloria and Phil certainly weren't the worst bosses. After the first week they'd left me to it most of the time.

I put one beer mat each on the two tables to the right of

the door. An old bloke called Danny would sit at one table and his mate Trevor would sit at the other. Everyone else would sit at the bar. There was a chance that someone else would come in and upset the status quo – it would be like a scene from a Western where everyone stops talking and turns around as the stranger walks into the saloon.

I'd been promised that things would be different during the season, so I thought I'd stick around to find out.

The holiday makers started to trickle in during Easter week, and Danny and Trevor started sharing a table to make way for the extra customers. The thing about seaside towns is that there are a lot of holiday flats all over the place and even back-street pubs like The Brown Bull enjoyed an influx of customers.

Rachel was part of that influx.

She came in one Saturday night in May. She was with two other girls and I noticed her as soon as they walked in. Paul, the part-time staff, was working that night and he'd served them their first round, but when I saw her stand up and gather the glasses I made sure that I was there to serve her when she reached the bar.

'What can I get you?' I asked.

'What are you offering?' she asked. She was flirting with me and I thought, *all right two can play at that game.*

'Your wish is my command,' I said, giving her my best smile.

She said that I could start by getting her three Bacardi and cokes.

Over the course of the evening I found out that her

name was Rachel and that she was here for a week with two friends to celebrate the end of their A Levels. They'd wanted to go to Benidorm but their budget hadn't run to it.

'What time do you finish?' she asked a couple of drinks later when the Bacardi had started to take effect.

I told her that I'd be finished around midnight. We couldn't compete with the pubs right in the centre of town so we closed at eleven and I was usually on my way home within the hour. Rachel's friends went on to a club after we closed, so she sat on a stool at the bar and waited for me.

Paul didn't object to having to clear up around her and Rachel and I left together when we were finished. I asked her if she wanted to go to a club or one of the other pubs in town but she said no. She said that she wanted somewhere more private, where we could get to know each other a little better. Ten minutes later she was unlocking the door to the rented flat that she was staying in. By the time I left, we knew each other very well.

It was after three when I walked the relatively short distance from Rachel's bed to Tanya's. It took me less than ten minutes. Tanya stirred but didn't wake up as I got undressed as quietly as I could and slid into the bed. I whispered that I was sorry but I don't think that she was awake enough to hear it.

I woke a few hours later to find an empty place in the bed beside me and I lay there for a few minutes listening to Tanya moving around in the kitchen next door. After a few more minutes the smell of bacon hanging in the air dragged me out of bed.

'Knew this would get you out of your pit,' she said as she moved bacon around the frying pan. 'Sit down, it'll be ready in a minute.' A few minutes later she put my breakfast in front of me. There was a mug of tea that I hadn't seen her make there too.

'Thanks,' I said. I waited for her to sit down with her own breakfast before I took the first bite. If nothing else, I have manners.

'I never heard you come in,' she said as she lifted her own sandwich from her plate.

'Good,' I pushed my food to the side of my mouth so that I could speak, 'that was the plan.'

She gave me a funny look so I explained that I hadn't wanted to wake her.

She left it at that.

Rachel wasn't the only casual relationship I had that summer. Who am I kidding? They weren't relationships, they were sexual encounters. Sex, pure and simple. No ties, no comebacks. I wasn't sure if Tanya knew what was going on but, if she did, she didn't say anything. Like that first night, the one after I'd slept with Rachel, Tanya might make a comment about me getting home late but she never asked where I'd been or who I'd been with.

Tanya wasn't a stupid woman – she must have known what was going on – she just chose not to say anything. To be fair, she could well have been sleeping with other blokes. I thought we had an open relationship that suited both of us. I suppose you'd call it friends with benefits.

TOM

By the time that Robert had been gone for about three months I was in love with Michelle and I couldn't imagine being without her. I also couldn't imagine how my brother could have walked away from her, but that was his loss.

We'd taken things pretty slowly by most people's standards, I suppose. We went out, I took her home and I kissed her goodnight. I'm not going to tell you that I didn't want things to go further – I'm no saint – but Michelle had been through so much and I didn't want to rush anything. That being said, we both knew how serious we were about each other.

I remember it was the May Day bank holiday Monday when I first went to Michelle's parents' house as her boyfriend. I'd met them before, but this time was different: before, I had just been Robert's younger brother.

I'd first suggested that we let our families know how serious we were the week before, but Michelle hadn't been so sure.

'Why not?' I asked.

She looked a bit sheepish as she said, 'My mum thinks I'm making a mistake.'

'Fair enough,' I told her, 'but it's your mistake to make.' Her eyes were wide as she looked at me. She looked so scared. 'Look, Michelle,' I took hold of her hands and tried to sound reassuring, 'you have to make your mind up. Either you're serious about me and about us or you're not and, if you *are* serious, then our families have to get used to it.'

So that's how I ended up sitting in the living room of Michelle's parents' house on a Bank Holiday Monday in May.

Conversation was a bit tricky. It was basically a question followed by a one sentence answer and then another question and so forth and so on. Michelle's mum had eyed me suspiciously when she'd handed me a cup of tea and her dad just eyed me suspiciously full stop.

I'd been there about an hour when Michelle's mum made some lame excuse to leave the room and took Michelle with her. I guessed that the moment of truth had arrived and it wasn't long before Davy Jenkins got to the point.

'Michelle's my only daughter,' he said, looking me squarely in the eye. 'Your brother has already broken her heart and I swear to God I could break his neck for doing that. If you hurt her,' he paused for effect before adding, 'rest assured, I will break yours.'

I matched the look he was giving me and told him, 'I am not my brother, Mr Jenkins.' We weren't on first name terms by that point and there would be a lot of water to go under the bridge before we were, but we had come to an understanding. We both loved Michelle.

A couple of days after that I told my parents that Michelle would be coming to the house.

'What's she coming here for?' Mum asked.

'To see me,' I said. I thought it was a pretty stupid question and I don't think I hid that fact from my voice.

'Why?'

There she was with another stupid question. 'Why do you think?' I asked.

I can't tell you how much effort it took not to laugh in her face when she said, 'Don't you take that tone of voice with me, Thomas!'

Oh no I thought, *not the Sunday title*. 'Well—' I didn't get chance to say anything else.

'Well what?'

Honest to God, I felt about five years old again. 'She was always welcome here before.' I said.

'And she's welcome now, son,' my dad said. Mum threw him a look that I couldn't see but he stood his ground. 'Yes she is, Janet,' he said firmly and I saw Mum visibly back down.

She stared at him for a few seconds and then turned back to me. 'I just don't understand what you think you're playing at,' she said, but the fight had gone out of her voice by then.

'I'm not playing at anything,' I said.

'She'll get the wrong idea, you know.'

I'm not even kidding, she really did say that. My mum has said many a stupid thing in her time, but I thought she'd excelled herself with that one.

'About what?' I asked.

'About what you want from her,' she spoke slowly,

emphasising each word.

I'd had enough of that conversation, so I told them that I was going to have a quick bath and left the room. 'She'll be here soon,' I told them just before I started to climb the stairs. But I didn't go upstairs straight away. I paused to listen to what my parents were saying to each other.

'Isn't it enough that she's ruined the life of one of our sons?' I heard Mum say.

'That's not fair, Janet,' Dad said quickly. 'Robert did wrong by her.'

I thought that Mum might be crying when she said, 'He was scared, that's all.' I heard her blow her nose before she said, 'And what's he going to think when he comes back and finds the two of them carrying on together?'

'He's not coming back, Janet,' Dad said.

Mum didn't disagree with him, at least not before I quietly climbed the stairs and went into the bathroom.

I made sure I was at the door to meet Michelle and I could tell that she was terrified at the thought of being here again. I put my arm around her shoulder and moved her gently through the door and into the house. She had done it unaided dozens of times before but she seemed to be finding it hard to get her feet moving that day. I didn't say anything to her, because I was fairly certain that my mum would have her ear to the door, but I tried to reassure her with a smile.

That first meeting between her and my mother, now that she was with me and not Robert, was a bit testy to say the least but Dad was really supportive. I knew that I had an ally in him.

I don't know if it was that conversation with my mother that set me thinking, but something did.

In my heart, I knew what I wanted my next step to be, but in my head, I couldn't help wondering why. My heart said that it was because I loved her but my head said that I barely knew her. My heart told me that I wanted to spend the rest of my life with her but my head reminded me that if Robert hadn't buggered off, Michelle and I would never even have had a date. A worm had buried itself into my mind and insisted on asking if I was still trying to be the brother that I had once idolised. Was I trying to be him by living the life that could have been his?

It kept me awake more than a night or two I can tell you, but in the end, I couldn't deny the way that I felt. I loved Michelle, pure and simple. I accepted that we hadn't got together in a conventional manner, but my feelings were real. I could spend the rest of my life questioning my motives or I could just go with my gut...

It was sometime in June, a warm summer's day, and we'd been out somewhere, I don't remember where. We were walking to the pub that used to be at the bottom of Hague Street; they stocked these nuts that Michelle really loved and she was craving them that night. That pub was the only place that we'd ever found them so we went there a lot. Anyway, we were walking there and I must have appeared as distracted as I was feeling, because Michelle asked me if I was all right.

'OK, I said to myself as I took a deep breath and prepared to jump in at the deep end.

'Michelle?' I stopped walking as I said her name and she walked on a step or two before she realised. When she turned around, she had a puzzled look on her face.

'What is it?' she asked.

'Will you marry me?' My voice was barely a whisper as I asked.

She was clearly surprised by my question and just stared at me. She didn't say anything and it was as if her eyes were asking me if she had heard me right. My stomach flipped and I thought that I had blown everything. I thought that I'd been kidding myself that we had a future.

'Why?' she asked. 'Why would you ask that?'

To tell you the truth, that wasn't the response I'd been hoping for, but I tried to laugh it off and said something like, 'Why do you think?'

She turned her head to the side and pouted. 'You shouldn't tease me,' she said,

'Who's teasing?' I asked. 'I've never been more serious.'

She turned back towards me and I watched as she scraped her lower teeth over her upper lip. Then she lifted her hands up and covered her face. I didn't know what to do. I'd thought that she'd... well, I suppose I'd *hoped* that she would feel the same way I did and say yes. I didn't know what was going on. I couldn't work out what she was feeling or thinking. She was breathing deeply and I saw her chest moving up and down. She seemed in distress and I was just about to reach out to her when she dropped her hands and I saw her face. Her eyes were wide.

'How can we?' she asked. 'How *can* we?'

She said it louder the second time.

She hadn't actually said no so I thought that I might be in with a chance as long as I could answer all of her questions. But first, I had one of my own. 'Why can't we?' I asked.

'Where would we live?' she asked, which struck me as on odd thing to say, but Michelle is nothing if not practical.

'We'll find somewhere,' I said. Finding somewhere to live seemed the least of our concerns.

There was a wall running along the gardens of the houses we were passing and she leaned against it. I did too. She looked at the ground between her feet and I watched her.

'*How* will we live?' she asked. 'I'm going to have to give up work soon.'

'I've got a job,' I told her.

'You have a job?' She sounded surprised and squinted her eyes to get a closer look at my face. 'A job as well as college?'

'Instead of college,' I said. She was the first person I'd told, and though I'd wondered if I'd done the right thing taking it, now I knew that I had.

She started to speak but she didn't get any further than, 'But...'

'But nothing,' I said. 'It's done. I start as a draughtsman

at Lodge's in a fortnight.'

She let the words sink in.

'Why, Tom?' she said the words quietly. 'Why do you want to *marry* me? Why would you want to marry *me*?'

'Why do you think?'. I started to wish that she'd just turn me down and put me out of my misery.

'But I'm pregnant,' she said.

I pushed myself away from the wall and took a couple of steps away so that I could gather my thoughts before turning around. 'Why does it always come back to that?' I asked. I said it louder than I meant to and Michelle seemed to flinch. I felt bad about that because it hadn't been my intention to sound harsh. I calmed myself down and said, 'It's a baby Michelle, not a spare head.'

She laughed at that, and then she smiled. She glanced away for a few seconds, then said, 'I wish...' but she left the sentence hanging.

'What?' I pushed her. 'What do you wish? Tell me what you're thinking, Michelle.'

I could see that she had started to shake and I wanted to put my arm around her but given that I had just asked her to marry me and she hadn't instantly said yes it felt awkward to say the least so I just stood and waited for her to tell me what she wished.

'I wish,' she said eventually, 'that things were different.' She spoke slowly and carefully. She opened her mouth to say something else but nothing came out. A couple of deep breaths later the words were there. 'I wish,' she paused and looked at me, 'that things could be the way you say they can.'

'They can,' I said, but she shook her head. 'They *can*, Michelle.' I felt like I was challenging her but I didn't care. I had to make her see things the way I did. '*Why* can't they be?'

'Because of the baby,' she whispered.

I remember putting my hands on my head in a gesture of exasperation. 'Can we forget about the baby for a minute,' I said.

'How can I?' Now it was she who sounded exasperated. 'How can I forget about it?' she gestured towards the bump on her stomach. She stifled a sob and I couldn't help but put my arm around her that time and bugger the awkwardness. Her face was buried in my shoulder but I could still hear her say, 'I don't want to be pregnant.'

'Let me look after you,' I whispered in her ear. 'Let me look after both of you.'

After about a minute or so she lifted her head and looked at me and said through a sniff, 'Ask me again.'

So I did. This time, she smiled and nodded her head as she said yes.

As we hugged, I saw a woman looking at us from the window of the house we were standing in front of. I thought she was about to tell us to get off her wall so I held my hand up to apologise, but she didn't say anything. She just looked and shook her head and disappeared. Either way I thought it best not to push our luck and I encouraged Michelle to move.

We made it to the pub eventually and that was where we

made plans for our future as Michelle sated her craving for honey roast almonds.

'What do you think they'll say?' she asked as we walked home. I didn't have to ask who 'they' were – I'd spent more than a minute or two thinking about it already.

'I really don't know,' I said. 'I doubt they'll think it's the best idea that either of us have ever had, but what does that matter?' I stopped walking and because she had her arm linked through mine she stopped too. It was quite funny at the time, because she had such a surprised look on her face as she realised her legs had moved but her upper body hadn't. I've not thought about that night in years but I can still remember that look on her face.

Her eyes were like saucers as she asked, 'What's wrong?'

There was nothing wrong – quite the opposite – it was just that even though it had been hours since I'd actually popped the question, and we'd spent those hours talking about it, the reality of what had happened only just hit me.

She had said yes. From now on the woman with those wide eyes and the surprised look on her face was going to be my priority and, as such, I would take care of her. I planned to spend the rest of my life looking after her; she would never have to face anything alone again.

That included her parents. We told them the following evening.

I don't suppose they'd given it much thought when Michelle got ready to go out, or even when I knocked on the door, but when Michelle took me into the living room

87

where her parents were watching the television, I could see the colour drain from her mother's face.

'Tom?' she made my name sound like a question.

I nodded a welcome to her and then one to her husband. Michelle grabbed my hand as she sat on the sofa, forcing me to sit down with her. I couldn't help but feel Michelle tense up beside me and when I glanced at her I could see that she was visibly shaking.

She opened her mouth but nothing came out, and when she looked at me I could see the fear return to her eyes. Then, after a couple of seconds, something changed and the fear turned to defiance. She took a deep breath, puffed out her cheeks and turned to her mother.

'Tom has asked me to marry him,' she said, 'and I've said yes.'

I could sense her dad moving in his chair and when I turned I saw that he had moved to the edge of his seat. 'What do you mean he's asked you to marry him?' he asked.

I thought it was pretty self-explanatory but I didn't think it was the time for sarcasm. Now, I can't remember who asked which question because they were both going at it. I felt like I was watching a tennis match because my head was going from side to side that much, and I can't remember the order they came in but, basically, the questions all came down to *why*?

I mean, they asked the practical things like where we would live and what would we live on, but basically it was all about the *why*?

After being interrogated for what felt like hours Michelle's mum went to make a cup of tea because, as we all know, that makes everything better – at least in a mother's world. Her dad fixed me in a steely stare.

'You know you don't have to do this don't you, son,' he said.

Well that's not patronising is it was another thought that I kept to myself, though I could see where he was coming from.

'I know,' I said simply.

I could see how uncomfortable he felt as he started to say, 'Just because it was your brother…'

I had to stop him before he went any further. 'I am not my brother's keeper, Mr Jenkins,' I said. 'I am not responsible for what he did and, while I hate what he did and I would kick his teeth in if he walked into this room right now, I am not doing this to make up for his actions. Nothing can make up for the pain that he caused Michelle,' – his face seemed to soften a bit at that – 'but something good came out of it.' I smiled at Michelle and put my arm around her shoulders. 'I got to know just how wonderful this young lady is and I want to spend the rest of my life with her.' God, the kids would retch if they heard me tell this story, but it was the truth and I wasn't afraid to say it.

I hadn't realised that her mum had come into the room in time to hear my speech. She didn't say anything but she did smile at me when she handed me my cup of tea. It was a breakthrough.

I'm not sure that they understood our motives for getting married, but by the time I left they had accepted that it was going to happen. Michelle stood on the doorstep with me as I prepared to leave.

'One down and one to go,' I said and she asked when we were going to tell my parents. We decided that the weekend would do

I opened the door to Michelle the following Saturday afternoon. Mum had scowled when I'd said that she was coming round, so you can imagine her face when I brought Michelle into the living room where she was sitting with my dad. I think she'd assumed we would be going out.

Dad looked up from the newspaper he was reading and said, 'Hello, love.' He folded the paper and put it on the arm of his chair.

'Hello, Mr Ellis,' she said in a shaky voice that told everyone that she was nervous about something.

Mum had been reading too – a book I think – which she put down as well. She aimed a sour look at Michelle as she sat next to me on the sofa.

'You all right, Mum?' I asked.

She transferred the look to me as she said. 'Fine thank you.'

'How are you keeping, love?' Dad asked. Now it was Dad's turn to get the look from Mum, but he didn't seem to notice and, if he had seen it, he certainly didn't care.

Michelle took a deep breath, 'I'm fine thank you, Mr Ellis,' she said. 'How are you?'

I'm willing to bet my life that Dad said 'Can't grumble,' because that was his standard answer whenever anyone asked him how he was.

There were no pleasantries coming from my mother so I took the bull by the horns, as it were.

'I've asked Michelle to marry me,' I said. I was speaking directly to my mother and she opened her mouth to say something but I got there first with, 'and she has said yes.'

Mum closed her mouth. She looked at Dad and so did I. He had one elbow on the arm of the chair and the other one on his knee. As he looked at us I swear I could see his support beaming towards us. It's like I've said before, I knew that we had an ally in him.

'Congratulations,' he said with a smile. 'I'm very happy for you.'

I let that sink in, enjoying the moment before I turned to my mum and waited for her to say something negative.

'You've only been going out for five minutes,' was all she had.

'Long enough,' I replied.

'But you're so young,' was her next offering.

'We're old enough,' I said. To be fair to her we were very young at twenty but, as far as I was aware, love wasn't just for the over twenty-fives or thirties or whatever age Mum deemed old enough.

'What do your mum and dad think about this, Michelle?' Mum asked.

'They're pleased for us,' she looked straight at my

mother as she answered her.

The three of us were shocked when Mum said with a sneer, 'I'll bet they are.'

Dad made a noise like he was going to say something, but he didn't get the chance because I asked first, 'What's *that* supposed to mean?'

I think even Mum was embarrassed by what she had said because she backed down and muttered, 'nothing.'

'We hope you'll be very happy,' Dad said after a moment or two of silence while he glared at his wife. Then there were a few more moments of silence before he made a point of saying, 'Don't we, Janet?'

She agreed that she did and for the rest of the time that we were there she made the right noises and said the right things but I knew it was for Michelle's sake. I was certain that she would have more to say to me when we were alone, and I wasn't wrong.

'Are you mad?' she asked when I got back from taking Michelle home.

'No,' I said flippantly. I know I shouldn't have taken such a dismissive attitude, but it was a ridiculous question.

She followed me into the kitchen and I could feel her eyes boring holes into my back as I filled the kettle. I switched it on and dropped a tea bag into the nearest mug. I put my hands on the worktop and leaned my weight on them. I knew that if I waited long enough she'd say what was on her mind.

I had to wait for a very long minute before she asked, 'Why?'

I didn't bother asking 'why what?' I just turned around slowly and said, 'Because I love her.'

'Have you got any idea how hard it will be?' she asked.

'I expect it's hard for any young couple getting married,' I said.

'It is,' she acknowledged, 'but it will be twice as hard for you.'

'Why will it?' I poured the water from the kettle into a mug as I spoke. I lifted the mug of steaming tea to my mouth and took a sip. It was too hot and I blew gently over the top of it. Mum was staring at me, so I asked her the question again. I know that I was goading her to a certain extent but I just wanted to get it over and done with.

'It'll be twice as hard, Thomas,' she explained, 'because she's having a baby.'

'I know she is,' I said.

'And it's not your baby,' she said. *Did she really think I didn't know that?*

'No, it's not,' I said defiantly, 'it's your other son's.'

'Rober— ' She started to say his name but couldn't get it out. She almost collapsed into the chair she'd been sitting on that day I'd found her looking at the note Robert had left. She put her elbows on the table and buried her head in her hands. 'Where is he?' she said.

I didn't know the answer and I didn't bother to guess.

Over the next few days Mum gradually seemed to come around to the idea. She'd probably realised that if she didn't, she would lose two sons.

A couple of weeks later, Michelle was lying on the sofa at her parents' house and resting her head on my knee. I was stroking her hair and I was happy. Her parents had gone to an old friend's birthday party or something and Craig was on holiday so we had the house to ourselves.

Up until that point our relationship hadn't moved much beyond kissing, but that evening the progression from the sofa to the bedroom was as natural as it was inevitable.

I'd been nervous enough but Michelle was even more so. I suppose she was worried about how I would react to the sight of her swollen belly. To be honest, I'd wondered myself how I'd feel when we were finally alone in the bedroom. I'd told everyone that the baby didn't make a difference but I'd known that that theory would be tested when I had nowhere to hide.

In the end I needn't have worried. She was beautiful and I told her so.

And, do you know what? When I lay there afterwards, with Michelle resting against my shoulder, I felt happier and stronger than I ever had before and I knew I was where I wanted to be and where I wanted to stay.

When we finally made love it was so good – well worth waiting for. Look, laugh if you want about a man getting soppy over his wife, but it really was incredible. We fell asleep afterwards and woke up in each other's arms. Total cliché I know, but that's just the way it was.

I woke up first and lay listening to Michelle breathing. She was making this little snuffly noise. Not a snore – for God's sake don't tell her I said she snored – just a little noise. I wondered if Robert had ever woken up here and listened to that noise. I forced myself to push that thought aside and reminded myself that Michelle and I were together now.

Robert was just part of the baggage that Michelle had. We all had baggage.

We were married nine weeks after I proposed. We could have waited until after the baby was born but we didn't want to. I didn't sleep much the night before the wedding. I spent most of it lying on my back looking at the shadows that the streetlight outside my window cast on the ceiling.

I loved Michelle and I knew that was why I wanted to marry her but I couldn't help asking myself why she would want to marry me. I believed her when she said that she loved me – I felt it – I just couldn't get rid of the little niggle that said it was because I reminded her of Robert. Was it Robert that she really wanted to marry?

My mum had implied more than once that Michelle's mother wanted to see her daughter married so that the baby wouldn't be born out of wedlock. I'd thought that was old-fashioned and ridiculous, but that night I wondered if she'd been right. More to the point, I wondered if that was why Michelle was marrying me.

Regardless of what might have happened in the past, times had changed. Girls didn't get married anymore just because they were pregnant. Michelle was a strong-willed woman and she was more than capable of bringing up a baby on her own if she chose to. But she hadn't chosen to do that. She had chosen to do it with me. She had chosen to marry *me*.

By four o'clock, I'd realised that I was being stupid and I managed to get a couple of hours sleep before it was time to get up.

Arranging a wedding so quickly meant that we had to get married at the rather obscure time, for those days anyway, of half eleven on a Wednesday morning. If we'd wanted a Saturday we'd have had to wait a long time.

'Who gets married on a Wednesday?' Mum had said when I told her the date.

'Don't know,' I said, 'but we are.' I'd half expected such a reaction so I was prepared for it.

'Nobody'll come,' she said, 'they'll be at work.'

'Well, we should save a bit on the champagne then, shouldn't we,' I replied.

She'd been drying dishes when I told her and she threw the tea towel down on the draining board at that point.

'Don't take that tone of voice with me, Thomas,' she said, 'because I'm getting a bit sick of it. I can't talk to you these days without you getting all sarcastic on me.'

I apologised for that because I could see that she was upset. I didn't want to upset her because she's my mother at the end of the day but, by that same token, I couldn't just let her get away with treating us that way.

As it happened, she wasn't wrong about the lack of guests at our wedding, and we ended up plighting our troth to each other in front of just twenty people. It didn't make a difference to me but I did wonder if Michelle was a bit disappointed. Isn't a big church wedding in a fancy frock what all girls dream of? She said that it didn't matter, but I wasn't sure. She said she was happy, so I had to take that at face value. Maybe we'd renew our vows one day and she could have the dress then.

I didn't have a brother around to ask, so I asked Craig to be my best man. He'd been surprised at first but seemed chuffed that I'd asked him and said yes. Of course, he might have agreed just so he could deliver one final message as we waited for Michelle and her dad to make the short journey from the door to the registrar's table.

He leaned over and whispered, 'Don't you dare hurt her, mate,' in my ear.

I didn't get the chance to answer because as the door opened, someone pressed play on the tape recorder and The Wedding March echoed around the room.

I'd had a meeting with the registrar before the service but had been ushered into the room we were getting married in as soon as the taxi containing Michelle and her dad had arrived outside. I'd sat with Craig and the assembled guests while Michelle had gone through the same process and when the music started to play I turned and got my first glimpse of her.

She took my breath away.

She moved towards me in a floaty pale pink dress with a flower in her hair and a smile on her face.

Five minutes later we were man and wife.

A small, hastily organised reception took place in the

function room of a nearby pub and, even though it wasn't the flashiest wedding most of them had been to, everyone seemed to have a good time. Someone described it as being a novelty. I think he was referring to the midweek wedding – you know, like it made a change from being at work.

Even my mother seemed to be enjoying herself which came as a pleasant surprise. To be fair to her, she had pretty much come around to the idea of the wedding by then, but I'd still had this dread at the back of my mind that she would do something to put a spanner in the works. I'd held my breath when the registrar had said the bit about anyone having an objection.

As Michelle and I prepared to leave our parents came towards us. It felt a bit like we were being tag-teamed. Michelle's parents reached us first and her mum threw her arms around her daughter and her dad came towards me with his hand outstretched. We shook hands firmly.

'Take care of my baby,' he said and I told him that I would.

Her mum gave me a hug then and said, 'Welcome to the family.'

They took a step or two back to allow my parents in. My dad shook my hand and patted my back while my mum kissed Michelle's cheek and appeared to whisper something in her ear. Then she kissed me quickly and told us to take care of each other. It might have been a trick of the light but I thought I saw a tear trickling down her face.

We waved goodbye to our guests and climbed into the

back of a taxi that would take us to a hotel for the night.

Michelle told me later that my mum had told her to take care of herself and the baby.

Talking of the baby, I got the phone call exactly three weeks later.

'I'm on my way,' I told Michelle and left the office with a mixture of nerves and excitement in my stomach.

I sat by Michelle's head and stroked her hair. Sweat had plastered it to her head but this was no time to be squeamish. She looked at me and pain was etched all over her face. I'd have given anything just to be able to take it away but there was nothing I could do other than hold a cup of rapidly melting ice-chips to her mouth.

We had been there for seven hours but finally the midwife emerged from Michelle's nether regions and said it was time. 'OK, Michelle,' she said, 'next time you feel the urge, I want you to push as hard as you can.'

The midwife had hardly got the words out before Michelle's face screwed up as she pushed. What seemed like only seconds later she was doing the same again. The midwife, and another nurse who had appeared from God knows where, urged Michelle on while I just prayed that it would be over quickly.

I got the shock of my life when the midwife – I think she said her name was Carol – said, 'Come on then, Dad, it's time,' and motioned with her finger for me to go to her.

I'd rather have stayed where I was, but I wasn't about to admit that. I looked at the place that the green sheet was covering and saw the baby's head. I don't know if I can explain exactly how it was that I felt then; it was a mixture of awe and wonder coupled with the need to faint. I put my hand on Michelle's knee and tried to speak but nothing came out so I patted her leg instead.

Carol – if that was her name – got into position and, one good push later, she was cradling the baby's head in her hands, manoeuvring the shoulders out and then grabbing the slippery little critter as it emerged.

It was a boy.

ROBERT

The season was pretty much finished by the middle of September. There were one or two stragglers stringing it out and making the most of the quiet, now that the screaming kids had all gone back to school, but for the most part it was just the people that lived there.

I thought my hours might get cut, or even finished altogether, but I got lucky. Turned out that Gloria and Phil were planning on retiring and wanted to find someone to manage the place. They asked me. I had nothing better to do, so I said yes.

'Guess that means that you'll be sticking around,' Tanya said when I told her.

'Suppose it does,' I said. Well, where else did I have to go? Anyway, it wasn't so bad. I had a job, somewhere to lay my head and a couple of girls who liked to spend the odd night with me. Not that they knew anything about each other.

Tanya and I celebrated with a takeaway and an early night.

Look I don't want to sound like a selfish prick but that's basically what I was back then. I had everything I wanted and I didn't give much thought to the life I'd left behind. There I was, Rob, the genial host of The Brown Bull who had an easy way with the customers and kept a good pint.

Back in my old life I'd been Robert, and even I didn't care much for him.

Robert's mother had always expected good things of him, things that I had no interest in achieving. Who wanted to be a solicitor like cousin Gerald anyway? Back there, Robert was the older brother, the responsible one that his kid brother looked up to, though God knows why. Back there, he was Robert the boyfriend, the one that had a pregnant girlfriend.

Why would I have wanted to go back to that? Robert was stifled but Rob was free. Like I said a selfish prick, and I knew it.

Selfish but not completely thoughtless. I didn't know when exactly Michelle would have been due to have the baby but once it got to the end of October I knew that her time would have come. I wondered what she had had and what she had called it. Traditionally, first-born sons in my family had been called Robert but, if the baby was a boy, I was pretty certain that she would have called it Lucifer before she gave it my name. I couldn't blame her for that.

Again, I thought of ringing her, but what would I have said? No, I'd left her behind, I'd left that life behind, and I had no intention of going back.

So I got on with my life.

TOM

I'm being totally honest with you when I say that I couldn't have loved that baby any more if he had actually been mine. He was my son, I know that, but you know what I mean: if I had actually fathered him. I looked at him and my heart soared.

Michelle and the baby were to be moved to a ward once they'd been given the all clear by the doctor so, while the examinations were happening, I went to the reception part of the maternity ward to use the pay phone to ring our families.

I rang her parents first and the telephone was answered on the first ring, which put an image in my head of them having sat by the phone for the last seven hours since I'd called them to say Michelle had gone into labour.

Her mum's voice was shaky as she said, 'Hello?'

'It's a boy,' I told her, and heard her give a little gasp.

'Oh my God,' she said and I could tell that she was crying by that point. 'Are they both all right?'

I told them they were fine, although Michelle was obviously tired, and that hopefully they were going to be moved to a ward shortly. She asked when they would be able to visit and I felt bad saying they'd have to wait until the following afternoon. It was getting late by then, so I told her I would ring in the morning to let them know which ward to go to.

'Tom,' her mum said. I heard her sniff and then she said, 'Thank you,' though I wasn't entirely sure what she was thanking me for.

I rang my parents next and it was Dad who answered the phone. We had a short conversation where he offered his congratulations and asked how they both were and then he told me that my mum would like to have a word.

She asked me the same questions that Dad had and I gave her the same answers, then she took a deep breath and said, 'Tom, will you please tell Michelle how happy we are?' I assured her that I would. 'Goodnight, son,' she added, 'see you soon.'

'Goodnight, Mum,' I said and, after the phone line had gone dead, I stood with the receiver in my hand just looking at it.

By the time I got back to Michelle she had had her check-up and so had the baby and they were being prepared to be moved to a ward. A porter turned up to push the bed that Michelle still lay on and, together with a nurse who carried the baby, I followed them to a lift and up a couple of floors to the maternity ward.

It was well past ten o'clock by that point so I had to leave them, though that was the last thing that I wanted to do. But it was a four-bed ward and two of those beds were occupied so it wouldn't have been fair to stay even if the nurses had allowed it. I stroked the baby's head and whispered, 'Goodnight, little fella,' and then I leaned over to Michelle. I kissed her and told her that I would be in to see her as soon as I could.

I was walking on air as I went down the corridor. The baby was here and they were both all right. I couldn't have been happier. As I drove back to the house that we were renting from Michelle's Uncle George and Aunty Paula the world looked like a different place – a better place.

A couple of hours later, I still hadn't gone to bed. I was sitting in a chair with a glass of whisky, reflecting on the conversation that Michelle and I had had the week before. We had spoken about the baby's birth certificate. I wasn't the natural father and therefore had no right to have my name on the certificate. It was disappointing but the law was the law at the end of the day. At first, Michelle had suggested stretching the truth and just putting my name in the box marked 'Father'.

'It'll have your genes, so why not,' she'd said.

Tempting as that was, we soon decided that obeying the law was probably the best option.

'But I want you to be the father,' she'd said.

'I will be,' I'd told her, 'in every way that matters.' We'd been sitting on the sofa in the living room and I pulled her closer to me with the arm that had been lying loosely over her shoulders.

'I know,' she'd said, 'but I want your name on the certificate.'

'And I will be,' I reminded her, 'it's just going to take longer.'

The plan was that I would legally adopt the baby and then my name could go on the certificate, but there was a process to go through and that was going to take the best part of a year. It would be worth the wait.

I went to bed eventually and slept better than I had in years.

The thought of being away from Michelle and the baby until the following night was like a punch to the gut, but at lunchtime the next day my boss came up to me and said, 'Bugger off and see that babby of yours.' I didn't need telling twice; I was out of there like a shot.

I got to the ward at the same time as Michelle's parents, and my mother-in law threw her arms around me in a big hug. She'd never done that before. I decided that maybe Michelle had been right when she'd told me one night that her mother thought I was a hero.

Strictly speaking it was only two visitors to a bed, but the nursing staff turned a blind eye to that particular rule and almost every bed we passed had at least three people sitting around it.

Michelle seemed pleased to see us all but our son couldn't have cared less and spent the whole time fast asleep in his crib. Did you notice there that I called him 'our son'? Even before we were married we had established that Michelle's child would be my child.

I stopped off at my parents' house on the way home from the hospital. I shouted, 'Hello, it's just me,' as I opened the door and I heard Mum's voice coming from upstairs. I thought it sounded like she was in Robert's old room but I couldn't be sure.

She came down the stairs with a duster in her hand and asked if I had been to the hospital. I told her I had.

'How's the baby?' she asked, and I told her that he was fine. She asked who he looked like and I said that he looked like a baby. I'm sorry, but what did she want me to say? That he looked like Robert? He was less than a day old for God's sake. His face looked like a prune. A beautiful prune, I grant you, but a prune is a prune at the end of the day.

'You can decide for yourself when you visit him,' I said and her face lit up at the prospect of that. She asked when that would be and I said that they could go that night.

If I'd thought that her face lit up when I'd suggested the visit it was nothing compared to what happened when she saw the little fella.

Michelle was propped up in bed with him in her arms as we walked in and Mum made a bee-line for him. She held her hands out in a 'Can I have a hold?' sort of gesture but Michelle looked past her to me and said, 'Sorry, but his daddy hasn't even had a hold of him yet.' Our eyes smiled at each other but I think we kept it off our lips.

I leaned in and kissed her. I asked her how she was as she slid our baby into my arms. I sat in the wing back chair beside the bed and watched my son fall asleep in my arms. Ten minutes or so later, Michelle suggested that my mother might like to hold her new grandson and I gently passed him over to her. Dad got in close and as they were billing and cooing over him Michelle and I shared a look. We had made our point.

Not long before the end of visiting time, Mum asked if we'd chosen a name for him. He was back in his crib by then and we all looked at him as if he was going to answer the question for us. In the end, his mum answered for him.

'Simon,' she said.

'But...' I think the word popped out without Mum realising it because she didn't continue with the sentence straight away. We all looked at her to see what was coming next and she tried to cover it up with, 'where does that come from?'

'Nowhere really,' Michelle said, 'we just like it.'

And that was the end of that.

We didn't mention that exchange until the following afternoon when we were alone. I had a fair idea what Mum had wanted to say and Michelle had worked it out too. Although I'd never known anyone who called him anything but Bob, obviously my father had been christened Robert after his father and grandfather before him. The baby's biological father had been called Robert after his father etc., etc. so maybe Mum had assumed that Robert's son would bear that name. Let me tell you, Michelle would have called that child Julie before she called him Robert.

'Was your mum all right about the name?' Michelle asked.

'She was fine,' I said which wasn't a lie, but as we'd walked back to the car park she had asked me again where the name had come from. I didn't tell Michelle that, though.

How would I have felt if Michelle had said she wanted to call him Robert? I would have been gutted but it was never an issue because she had told me early on that she planned on calling the baby Simon if it was a boy. Had it been a girl she would have called her Hannah.

Back in the eighties it wasn't like it is now when you can be in and out the same day that your baby is born. Mothers of first babies spent the best part of a week in hospital, which gave me plenty of time to get everything perfect for when I brought Michelle and Simon home.

Four weeks to the day after we were married, we brought our baby home. Our neighbours that we barely knew came to the door as we pulled up in the car.

'You all right, love?' the woman, Janice asked. Michelle said that she was fine. Janice said that she and her husband Keith would see us later, 'after you've settled in like.'

We went to register the birth a couple of days later and the plan had been to do it together but the weather had other ideas. It had been overcast when we left the house but by the time we got into town it was belting it down with rain and blowing a gale. I stayed in the car with the baby while Michelle went into the register office alone.

I watched Michelle walk away and then turned my attention back to Simon who I was cradling in the crook of my left arm. This was the first time that we'd actually been alone together and it was a special moment. It was time for a man to man chat.

It went something like this: 'Hello, little fella, I'm your daddy and I'm going to look after you. I am going to look after you for ever and I promise that I will always be there for you.'

I think that was when I lowered my head and kissed him. He smelled of a mixture of soap and baby powder. 'I'm your daddy and I love you,' I told him again, just in case he hadn't understood me the first time. He fell asleep in my arms and I watched the rain roll down the windscreen. I was smiling.

My mind was miles away and Michelle startled me when she climbed back into the car. She leaned over and kissed me. 'Let's go home,' she said and by the time that I'd parked the car outside our house the sun was shining.

When we were in the house Michelle took Simon's outer layers off and put him down in his cot. He didn't so much as open an eye during the whole process. We left the room and I closed the door carefully behind us. Michelle asked if I'd like a coffee and I said that I would. She took a brown envelope from her bag and placed it in a drawer along with lots of other stuff that we didn't know what to do with. 'It's not the real one,' she said. 'When we get the real one, that one's getting burned.'

We got the real one after we'd jumped through various hoops for almost ten months. Even though everyone who loved him thought of him as an Ellis, Simon had officially been a Jenkins. In the August after he was born he became Simon Ellis and in the space that had previously had the word 'Unknown' written in it, his father was listed as Thomas Ellis: me. I had legally adopted him. Even though I'd acted the part for almost a year I was now the legal father of Robert's son.

Michelle was true to her word and, when we got home, she rummaged through the drawer, pulled out the brown envelope, held it over the sink and set fire to it. She dropped it and once it was entirely gone she turned on the tap and washed the ashes away.

I was holding Simon during this process and he bounced up and down in my arms as he watched the flames. He slapped me across the face with his flailing hands and giggled. He seemed as happy as we were.

Our parents had known what was happening that day and Michelle's dad, who I was now calling by his first name, Davy, had suggested a celebration but Cathryn, his wife, had said that might not be such a good idea. I realised that she'd been thinking of my Mum's feelings and I thanked her for that. Mum was still missing Robert and there was no need to rub her nose in it.

Anyway, we wanted to celebrate as a threesome.

When I say 'celebrate' I mean we wanted to just spend some time together as our own family unit, I did however speak to my dad about it a few days later. It was a Saturday and Michelle had gone shopping with her mum and taken Simon with her. They were looking for a birthday present for Michelle's grandma, as I recall. Anyway, I was at a loose end so I'd asked my dad if he wanted to go for a pint and he didn't need asking twice.

He went to the bar when we got there, and I found a table. He carried the beers back to the table and set them down before sitting on the stool beside me. Our shoulders were touching. We didn't say anything to each other for the first few minutes, preferring instead to sip our beer in silence. Then Dad set his glass on the table and started fiddling with it. He held it at the bottom and twisted it from side to side. I had a feeling he had something on his mind.

'It was a good thing that you did, son,' he said without taking his eyes off the glass.

I knew what he was talking about, but I didn't say anything, not because I didn't know what to say but because I didn't think it needed saying.

'I'm proud of you, Tom,' he lifted the glass to his mouth and added, 'which is more than I can say for your brother,' before he took a large gulp of his beer. After he'd put the glass back down he said it again. 'It was a good thing that you did.'

'Not really,' I told him. 'I only did what I wanted to do.'

'Yes, but it's not everyone who would take on another man's child.' He'd obviously taken some air in as he drank his beer because he was fighting to control a burp as he spoke.

'Yes, well, he's not another man's child now, is he?' I said it a bit more harshly than I'd meant to and I mouthed the word 'sorry', but Dad shook his head to say it wasn't necessary.

'You are happy though, aren't you?' He tossed his head back and emptied the contents of his glass.

I smiled and said, 'I'm married to Michelle,' before emptying my own glass.

Dad smiled. 'Good point,' he admitted as he picked the

glasses up and made his way back to the bar. I started to protest that it was my round but he was away before I got the words out of my mouth. I watched him as he stood at the bar. He was chatting casually to the man beside him as he waited his turn to be served. I'd always had a good relationship with my dad and I hoped that I would have a similar one with my son.

My son, I said it again in my head just because I liked the sound of it.

As Dad came back from the bar I told him that it was my turn next and he made a noise that more or less told me to shut up. As he put a glass in front of me I asked how my mum was.

'Much the same,' he said as he sat down. 'She's happy for you, though,' he said between sips, 'and she's happy about you adopting Simon.'

I knew she would be, because as long as 'Father unknown' remained on Simon's birth certificate she was probably scared that her grandson would be snatched away from her. There was no denying that she loved Simon and, now that I was listed as his father, she would always be his grandma regardless of what happened between Michelle and me.

ROBERT

That first Christmas was a bit weird.

Normally I'd spend most of the time between the 23rd of December until the day after New Year half cut, starting with the 'works do' that always began about ten minutes after we closed the garage for the Christmas break and finished after we'd brought in the New Year.

I'd been with Michelle the year before, but that hadn't stopped me from having my fair share of alcohol. Well, I was off work so why not make the most of it?

That first Christmas after I left home it was just the opposite. I spent most of the time working and barely had a drink at all. On Christmas Day, I was at the pub before ten so that I could set the bar up. We weren't doing food or anything, but Gloria had said that there would be more than enough in for a lunch-time pint to make it worth opening. I'd had my doubts, but it turned out that Gloria knew what she was talking about: the first customer came in before I'd even got back to the bar after opening the door.

Soon the place was half full of men trying to get away from the cooking of the Christmas dinner. I can't remember who said it now, but the place was in uproar when someone said that 'the wife's had the bloody Brussels on since before breakfast!' Someone else said they'd come to get away from the kids and another that they'd escaped before the in-laws turned up. There was a camaraderie about them.

I enjoyed that shift because they were all in a good mood, which made them generous: most of them put a pint for me behind the bar.

I went home to my own Christmas dinner after closing time. Remember, this was back in the days when pubs were only open for a few hours in the afternoon and then again in the evening so I was back at Tanya's flat by quarter to four and the bird was on the table shortly after that. We didn't have a turkey, it seemed a bit pointless just for the two of us and to be honest I'm not that keen on it anyway. I think we had chicken.

As we sat there opposite each other, wearing the paper hats that had come out of the crackers Tanya had insisted we pulled, I couldn't help thinking back to all the Christmases that had gone before, the one's where we had opened presents after breakfast and Mum made enough food to feed an army. I tried not to dwell on it, because that wouldn't have been fair on Tanya who had made an effort to make a nice meal and create a festive atmosphere. We'd decided to open our presents after we'd eaten the Christmas pudding.

I think I bought her some perfume and she got me a jumper. The meal had been nice, but I've got to say that I wasn't exactly full of Christmas cheer. I think that was when I missed my family the most. I didn't miss them enough to ring them, though.

I was working New Year's Eve too, so Tanya came with me and sat at the end of the bar. There were lots of girls in that night and more than one of them gave me the eye, if you know what I mean, but I was sure to make Tanya the first person I kissed at midnight. We both knew that I wasn't faithful to her, but I wasn't going to rub it in her face: despite what you might think I'm not a complete bastard.

She helped me clear up after the punters had all gone home. 'Made any resolutions?' she asked as she gathered glasses.

'No,' I looked up from the table that I was wiping. 'What's the point? I don't smoke, I'm not overweight and I don't drink much these days.'

She laughed at that. Tanya had a lovely laugh and her face sort of creased up into a ball. I got the feeling there was something else she wanted to say to me but she couldn't bring herself to get whatever it was off her chest. A couple of times I noticed her open her mouth as though she was going to say something, but she stopped herself when she realised I was looking at her and forced a smile onto her face.

Once I had locked up, we walked the short distance home. It wasn't far and I thanked God for that because it was freezing; a frost was forming and we could see our breath as we spoke. Not that we spoke about anything much, not while we were walking home anyway. That was saved until we were back in the flat.

Tanya opened a bottle of whisky and poured some in a glass that she handed to me. She poured some into a second glass and I couldn't help noticing that she'd poured herself a healthier measure than she had given me.

She held the glass up in a toast and said, 'Happy New Year, Rob.'

I held my glass up too and said, 'Happy New Year, Tanya.'

She was acting oddly so I wasn't surprised when she said, 'We need to talk.'

'Sounds serious,' I tried to make it light-hearted.

She didn't laugh or even smile. She just looked at me and nodded towards the empty chair opposite the one that she had lowered herself into. She set the whisky bottle on the coffee table between us.

Do you know what went through my mind? I thought *shit, she's pregnant*. I sat and waited.

I didn't have to wait long. Just long enough to drain half the whisky she had left.

'I've made a resolution,' she said eventually.

'OK,' I stretched the word out in that way you do when you really want to say *what the hell are you talking about?*

'Yes,' she emptied the glass, picked up the bottle and poured herself another generous measure. She looked at the glass for a couple of seconds before she looked up and said, 'I've resolved to put myself first this year.'

Call me stupid if you like but I didn't know what she was getting at so I said, 'Good idea.'

'I'm not going to put up with second best anymore,' she said, 'and I'm not going to put up with *being* second best.'

That was when the penny dropped. I reached over, pulled the bottle towards me and refilled the glass that I hadn't yet emptied. I wasn't a massive whisky fan back then, but any port in a storm.

'I know what you've been doing, Rob,' she said, 'and I'm not prepared to put up with it anymore.' She made a noise that sounded like a laugh, 'I know we're no Romeo and Juliet but I thought that we had something.' She drained her glass again but she didn't refill it this time. She put the glass on the table and looked at me. 'I'm going to bed now,' she said slowly, 'and I don't expect you to be here when I get up in the morning.'

She walked towards the bedroom and opened the door. She started to go in but stopped short and turned around again. 'I don't hate you Rob, it's just that I'm too long in the tooth to be lying in bed at night waiting for you to come home from shagging whoever the hell it is you've been with. We just need different things, that's all.'

I can still see her there, silhouetted against the dim light inside the bedroom with her head turned looking at me over her shoulder.

'I'll still talk to you if I see you in the street,' she said as she leaned down to pick up something that had been sitting on the bedroom floor. It was the bag that I had brought with me when I left home. By the sound it made, it was already packed.

'Make sure that you put your key through the door after you've locked it.' She closed the bedroom door behind her.

I looked at the door until the light that seeped between the frame and the hinges was switched off. I sat back in the chair and considered my options. About half an hour later I was back in the pub, or rather in the flat above it. Gloria and Phil had lived there but it had been empty since they'd buggered off to Tenerife. Gloria had said that it was mine if I wanted it and I realised that she had probably seen this day coming.

I thought about moving on after Tanya threw me out, you know, throwing my bag in the back of the car and setting off into the sunset, but in the end, I decided to stay where I was.

I had a job that I was actually starting to enjoy and somewhere to live that cost me next to nothing in rent. I liked being Rob and other people liked Rob too. Well, maybe not Tanya at that point, but that wasn't reason enough to start again.

I'm kidding about Tanya, by the way. I think she was pretty much OK with me right from the start. She popped into the pub the Saturday after New Year to drop off some stuff that I'd not taken with me. I saw her come in and she sort of smiled at me so I figured she hadn't come for a row. She found herself a spot at the end of the bar and, after I'd finished with the person I was serving, I joined her. I asked her if she was all right and she said that she was.

'Can I get you a drink?' I asked.

'Yes, and make it a double,' she said without hesitation.

I placed a double Bell's in front of her and said, 'It's on me.'

She actually said, 'Thanks,' but I could tell that what she really wanted to say was that it was the least that I could do. She took a sip of her drink and then deposited the carrier bag she was carrying on the bar. 'Thought you might want these,' she said.

I thanked her and put the bag under the counter without looking at what was in it. I'd realised that I was missing a shirt and some underwear so I didn't need to look. I didn't know whether to feel pleased that I had one of my favourite shirts and pair of Y-fronts returned, or disappointed that Tanya had wanted every trace of me out of her flat as soon as possible.

I didn't dwell on it.

By the time Tanya left, two double whiskies later, we'd agreed that it had been fun and we would remain friends.

TOM

I'd be lying if I said that I didn't think of Robert from time to time, and there was one time when I couldn't help but laugh. I wasn't laughing *at* him though, but at myself and the way I'd been during all the years that we grew up together when I was striving to be like him: when I'd wanted to be confident like him; when I'd wanted to be popular like him – essentially, when I had wanted to *be* him. I laughed because I realised that I was now living his life, or at least the one that he could have been living. And do you know what? It felt amazing.

Sometimes, especially in the early days, I knew that Michelle was thinking about him too. It was understandable I suppose. She never said anything, but there was something in her eyes that gave her thoughts away.

We had a party on Simon's first birthday. Well, party might be a stretch, but we had a cake. Michelle made it in the shape of a car and she used sliced Swiss roll for the wheels. I can still see Simon with a fistful of cake in each hand and a big grin on his face. Obviously, he hadn't a clue what was going on. He was just happy.

It wasn't long after that birthday that my mum put her foot in it. It wasn't the first time that her foot had been in whatever 'it' was but it was the biggest *faux pas* she'd made to that point.

We'd gone around to my parents' for Sunday lunch and after we'd eaten we were all in the living room chatting while we had a cup of coffee. Simon was on Mum's knee and he was gurgling as she chatted to him. It was just the usual sort of thing, you know *who's a lovely boy then* and that sort of thing, but then she said, 'You're the spit of your daddy.'

You could have heard a pin drop.

It wasn't that we'd been listening to what she was saying in particular but we all heard that comment and we all, as one, looked at her.

'Janet,' Dad mumbled.

'What?' Mum's voice was raised and you could see her expression change. The colour seemed to drain from her face as she realised what she had said. She quickly regained herself. 'Well he is,' she said, nodding her head towards me. 'He's the image of Tom.'

I've chosen to believe that that was what she had meant all along, but another part of me thinks that it was just lucky for her that I look so much like Robert.

Michelle wasn't quite so forgiving and within minutes she was making noises about leaving.

'Are you OK?' I asked her as we walked home. She was pushing the pram where Simon was now sleeping soundly and I was walking beside her with my hands in my pockets.

'I'm fine,' she said but in a way that really meant that she was anything but fine. She walked on a couple of steps and stopped without warning which meant that I walked past her. When I turned around she was looking into the pram.

'What's wrong? I asked.

She didn't say anything at first. She leaned in towards Simon and pulled his blanket away from his face. I looked at him too. He was moving his lips as he slept and dribbling down his chin.

'He does look like you, doesn't he?' she said.

'Poor bugger,' I laughed and that made her laugh too.

When Simon was about eighteen months old, Michelle told me that she was pregnant again. We were sitting on the sofa in our living room and Simon was playing on the floor in front of us.

I didn't say anything immediately because I wanted to take a second just to get the idea of it straight in my head. And then I smiled.

Later, in bed, while Michelle was sleeping beside me, I lay on my back and stared at the ceiling. I'd been staring at it so long that, in spite of the dark, I could clearly see all the little cracks that had been there since... well, since as long as we'd been there. We'd mentioned it to Michelle's aunt and she'd said that she would get it checked out but somehow she'd never got around to it.

I replayed the scene where Michelle had told me she was pregnant over and over again in my head, and every time I did it felt as good as it had the first time. I asked myself how it was possible that Robert had not felt this way when Michelle had told him that she was expecting. It was amazing. I tried to imagine the feeling that would make me up sticks and leave everything behind, but I couldn't.

Robert had been gone for just over two years by then and – other than thinking he was a stupid sod – I hadn't actively thought about him much in recent months. I thought about him a lot that night though.

I eventually went to sleep and woke just before seven to the sound of Simon crying in the next room. I started to get up but Michelle, as always, was up first. It was like she was expecting his crying to happen and was ready for it. The alarm was due to go off in three minutes so I lay where I was and waited.

While I waited my eyes were drawn once again to the crack in the ceiling. I know Paula had said that she would get around to fixing it but she had shown no signs of doing so, maybe now that there was another baby on the way it would be the perfect time to start looking for a place of our own. We didn't have a lot of money but whatever we had left at the end of the month we saved and that, added to the bit I'd managed to save when I was younger, might be enough for a deposit on a house. It wouldn't be a mansion but it would be ours.

I suggested it to Michelle over breakfast and while she was all 'can we afford it?' and that sort of thing, I'd seen the light in her eyes and that told me she was keen.

'It wouldn't be much,' I told her, 'but it'll be a start.'

I made an appointment to see the bank manager a couple of days later. We were in luck because he explained that they did something called a hundred per cent mortgage which meant that we didn't need a deposit at all. They don't do that sort of thing now so I guess those of us who bought our first homes in the eighties were lucky. I wouldn't like to think that I had to come up with a deposit for a house these days. They gave mortgages out like sweets back then, so once I'd proved that I had a regular income that was that.

Anyway, going on my salary, he offered us a fifteen thousand-pound mortgage and Michelle set about looking for houses like a woman possessed.

We spent the next few weekends looking in estate agents' windows and viewing houses. One or other set of grandparents looked after Simon while we spent hours trying to find what we were looking for. I thought we'd found it on Elm Avenue until we went to view the house and Michelle took an instant dislike to the woman selling it. There was nothing rational about her reaction and, if I asked her what her issue with the woman was, Michelle couldn't have told me but it was enough to stop us putting in an offer. To be honest I didn't much fancy it either, but that had more to do with the state of the back garden than anything else.

So, we kept on looking.

A few weeks after that viewing we went to see a house on King Street and as soon as we walked in we both knew that we had found what we were looking for. It had a decent sized living room and kitchen downstairs, with the bathroom, a biggish bedroom, and two smaller bedrooms upstairs. There was a small garden to the front and a slightly larger one to the rear and we'd felt at home as soon as we walked in. We could see our furniture sitting in the rooms and we could imagine what the children's rooms would be like, with colourful walls and toys on the floor.

The price was within our budget and the best thing of all was that the vendors already had a house that they had moved into and had essentially been paying two mortgages for six months, so they were as keen as we were to make the deal. I rang the estate agent on the Monday morning, the offer was accepted by lunchtime and that evening, once Simon was safely tucked up in bed, Michelle and I started making plans.

We moved in at the end of July. The decorating might not have been to our taste but we decided we could live with it and change things as we went along, so we moved in and started to make the house into our home. Michelle has a real flair for that sort of thing and had the place looking great in no time.

Simon's room already had white walls so they were easy to paint with very little preparation. It was the same in the smallest bedroom, the one that would be the nursery, which we painted in a pale yellow sort of colour. These days, new parents get to know what the sex of their baby is but back then babies were a surprise, so we had to go for something that we could adapt.

That first Christmas in our own home was amazing. You should have seen Simon's face when Michelle brought him into the living room the morning after we'd stayed up till one o'clock trimming the tree and decorating the room with streamers and balloons.

I'd gone downstairs and switched on the tree lights and I was ready with a camera to catch his reaction. It was priceless. The poor kid actually stopped breathing for a second. We didn't have much money to spare but what we had went on buying presents for Simon.

Michelle went into labour on the first Wednesday in January.

I was still on holiday until the following Monday so I was there when it started this time. Michelle calmly explained to Simon that he was going to visit Granny Jenkins while she went to the hospital to 'get the baby'. I don't think he understood that but he was happy enough to go to Granny's.

Michelle was a bit teary on the way to the hospital. She hadn't liked leaving Simon. I told her that he'd be fine but it didn't seem to make any difference.

Her second delivery was much quicker, and just three hours after getting to the hospital she was holding our second son in her arms. He was healthy, he was perfect, and I was the happiest man in the world.

It was after eight when I got to my in-laws and Simon was already in the bed that Michelle's parents kept at their house. We didn't get many nights out, but on those rare occasions that we did, Cathryn and Davy would babysit for us.

While Cathryn made me something to eat I crept into the bedroom, knelt down by the bed and looked at Simon through the bars of the guard rail. His lips were pursed and though his eyes were closed they were moving. I reached over and stroked his soft blond hair.

'You've got a little brother, mate,' I told him.

Davy suggested that I stay the night and I accepted without hesitation. I wanted to be there when Simon got up in the morning.

I slept well on the sofa and woke up to the sound of 'Daddy!' being squealed in my ear. I pretended to be asleep and I felt Simon climbing onto the sofa. I grabbed him and he giggled. I lifted him onto my chest and we lay with our faces just inches apart. I told him about his baby brother, but I don't think he really understood what it meant until I took him to the hospital that afternoon. Michelle's parents waited outside the ward while I took Simon in. He ran to the bed where his mum was holding his baby brother in her arms.

'He started to cry,' Michelle said, as if she was apologising to Simon for having someone else in her arms.

'See, see,' Simon said and he stood on his tiptoes to try and get a glimpse of what she was holding.

I took his shoes off and lifted him onto the bed so that he could get a closer look.

'Who that?' he asked.

I sat on the bed too, pulled Simon onto my knee and said, 'That's your baby brother.'

He had a puzzled look on his face as he looked at the newcomer and then he did the sweetest thing. He pushed himself off my knee, leaned over and kissed the baby.

It was our first moment together as a family.

Simon and I brought them home from hospital two days later. As Michelle carried the as yet unnamed baby out to the car, Simon carried a teddy bear that Michelle had taken to hospital with her. She'd read somewhere that it would help to avoid jealousy.

As it turned out we didn't need to worry. Simon never appeared jealous of the baby Anthony. We were careful to make a fuss of Simon – we didn't want him feeling left out – but the truth is, he took to his role of big brother like a duck to water. He would go and get nappies for his mum and wave toys at Anthony to try to make him laugh. However, I always made sure that when I got home from work I gave Simon a hug before I went to see the baby. We wanted him to know that he was still as important as he had always been.

We settled down as a family unit and life was good. I had a wife that I loved and two beautiful children.

I think it was in the November after Anthony was born that we decided to take the boys to a professional photographer for a portrait. We took them along one Saturday morning and the photographer, a prematurely grey-haired man wearing a garish green shirt, set the boys up on a sheepskin rug in front of a blue background. He chatted away to them as he clicked his camera, using toys and props to get the boys to smile.

'There's no mistaking them for brothers,' he said as he moved from one knee to the other so that he could get a different angle. 'They're like two peas in a pod.'

He was right, they were.

A week or so later, I watched as Michelle placed a parcel on the kitchen table and carefully pulled tape away from the brown paper that was covering it. I looked over her shoulder as she lifted one of the portraits up and looked at it. Her hands started to shake and she rested the frame on the table top. She stroked the image of Simon as he smiled out from the canvas and then she did the same to Anthony's.

I put my hands on her shoulders and asked her what was wrong. She said that she didn't know. She laid the frame down flat and turned around so that she was facing me. She wasn't sobbing or anything but I could see a couple of wet trails on her cheeks.

'Thank you,' she said, though I didn't know what for. 'For everything,' she explained and I hugged her and told her not to be daft.

Later, when the boys were in bed and Michelle was having a bath, I sat in the living room and thought about what had happened. What had she meant when she thanked me for everything? Did she mean for agreeing to the photo shoot that I hadn't been sure about? I thought probably not. The reality was that I was the one who should have been thanking her.

I was still going over it when Michelle came into the room wearing a terry towelling dressing-gown and a towel around her head. I held my arm out and invited her to join me on the sofa. She sat down, curling her feet beneath her and resting her head on my chest.

'You know when you thanked me earlier on,' I said, 'well… it's me that should have been thanking you.' She didn't say anything but she did push herself further into my side. I kissed the top of her head but I doubt she felt it through the towel. 'You and those two little fellas upstairs are my world.'

She pushed herself up and with her face close to mine said, 'I love you so much, Tom,'

We made love on the sofa.

ROBERT

I spent my twenty third birthday alone in my flat and, as I sat there nursing a glass of single malt that I'd brought up from the bar, I had nothing else to do other than think about my previous birthday: the night Michelle had told me she was pregnant.

The following day it would be a year since I'd got in my car and driven away from everything and everyone that had ever meant anything to me. Did any of it mean anything to me now?

Of course it did. There were days when I could've killed for one of Mum's steak and kidney pies, or gone for a pint with my dad even though he did go on a bit sometimes. I even missed my kid brother from time to time.

Tom was a good lad at heart, a bit like a puppy sometimes – you know, hanging around for any crumbs that you might throw him – but I liked him. Poor bugger had spent all of his life wanting to be me but I was willing to bet that wasn't the case anymore. I thought he was probably the golden child now, the one that could do no wrong, the one that didn't do a runner as soon as he got a lass in the family way.

I know that he had wanted to be me but, the ironic thing was that sometimes I wanted to be more like him. There was a reason that I'd asked him to keep a look out for Michelle, and that was because I knew that he would. I was willing to bet that he was the best uncle a kid ever had.

I drained the best part of half a bottle of whisky that evening and I don't remember how I got to bed.

The second season that I was at the pub passed in pretty much the same way as the first one except that I knew what to expect, my job was more secure, and I was living alone so I could sleep with whoever I wanted to without worrying about it. Not that I ever really worried about Tanya, but you know what I mean.

Do you know, this is the first time that I've ever put what happened into words and I realise how bad it makes me look. I wasn't a nice person. I'd done Michelle and the kid a favour.

There's not a lot to tell about my early twenties: I went to work and I had casual sex with a lot of women. I knew it was a dangerous game I was playing because you have to remember that this was back in the days when hysteria about AIDS was at its height. I watched those adverts with the gravestone on them and I knew that I had to be careful, but careful to me meant a condom, not abstention, and luckily for me there were enough girls around that felt the same way.

I spent two years living that way. And then I met Diane.

Diane came into the bar one evening in the third summer after I'd left. What we euphemistically called the function room had been booked for a seventieth birthday party and Diane was the grand-daughter of the birthday girl. I popped into the room a couple of times during the evening to check that everything was all right and I'd noticed Diane almost as soon as I'd gone in the first time. She was the only one dancing on the tiny dancefloor and I smiled at her when she looked my way.

She was standing at the bar the second time that went in, and she said hello when I checked on Danny who was working the bar in that room. She must have heard him call me by name because she used it as I walked away and I turned around.

She smiled at me and from that point I was putty in her hands.

Diane was different to the girls I normally went out with. I found that my sole intention of seeing her wasn't to get her into bed, and that scared the hell out of me. I enjoyed her company and I liked being with her. We slept together, but not until we had been going out for a couple of months. Not counting Michelle, it was the first time that had happened to me.

Diane moved in with me a couple of months after that and we settled into life together. From time to time I would think that this was how things could have been with Michelle but it wouldn't have been the same really, would it? If I'd stayed and settled down with Michelle there would have been a baby to consider. There would have been a baby tying me to her. Nothing tied me Diane: even though she shared the flat above the pub with me, there was nothing to keep her there if things didn't work out.

Things worked out pretty well for a while, but after six or eight months I could sense a sea-change with Diane. When we were out shopping she would slow down as we passed jewellers' shops and eye the rings in the window. She would say that she was looking at earrings or something but she wasn't and it seemed like one or other of her friends was getting engaged every other week.

We split up before Christmas.

Angela came to work at The Bull the following year.

She'd turned up for her interview wearing a pair of jeans and a tight red T-shirt so she immediately stood out from the two people I'd seen before her who had both turned up dressed like they were going to a funeral, you know, dark business suits. They were after a job in a back-street pub for God's sake, not a bank.

I call it a back-street pub but, without making it sound like I'm blowing my own trumpet, it had come on a lot since Gloria and Phil had handed the reins over to me. I'd sorted out the back room, which had been little more than a store room before, and turned it into the function room that I told you about. We'd started to do more food, which was bringing in extra revenue, and I'd renegotiated with the brewery which meant that the margins were better. All right, I *am* blowing my own trumpet, but why the hell not? I was good at my job.

Anyway, getting back to the point, we were taking on extra staff and Angela stood out from the other two. Her first shift was a Wednesday evening and after we'd locked up we tidied up and I asked her if she'd like a coffee or something. She laughed and suggested that we should probably have done that before we'd loaded the dirty dishes into the dishwasher.

'I've got cups upstairs,' I told her.

Would you believe me if I told you that we drank coffee and talked? You should, because it's the truth. She was so easy to talk to and she seemed to want to talk as much as I wanted to listen. She had long blonde hair and a figure that most girls would kill for and so I don't suppose she was used to blokes just wanting to talk to her.

'You not from round here, are you,' she said. It was a comment, not a question, something that she was certain of and I guessed that my accent was a giveaway.

'No,' I admitted as I handed her a mug of instant coffee. She didn't strike me as a coffee snob so I didn't think she'd mind. She had cosied herself into the corner of the sofa with her feet tucked underneath her. I noticed that she'd kicked her trainers off and made herself at home. She took a sip of her coffee and smiled as if it was the best thing that she had ever tasted.

She asked things like, 'How long you been here?' and, 'Do you like it?' before she asked the sixteen-million-dollar question of, 'Why did you come here?'

How to answer that one? I shrugged my shoulders to give myself a bit of thinking time and decided to tell her, 'There was a traffic jam on the A1.'

She did that thing with her eyebrows where they almost join in the middle, what's it called, furrowing? I smiled to myself because I thought my answer was clever. Needless to say, she asked what I meant.

'I wasn't sure where I was going,' I said, 'but I was on the A1 and there was a traffic jam. I sat there for a while and then I realised that the turnoff to here was just up the road so I nipped onto the hard shoulder, turned right at the roundabout, and here I am.'

She sipped her coffee and studied me a while. 'What made you leave?' she looked me straight in the eye though I noticed that her head was tilted slightly to one side.

I thought carefully before I answered.

'There was nothing for me there.' It wasn't like I was lying to her but I wasn't ready to tell her the truth, not the whole truth anyway. She asked me if I had a family and before I'd realised what I was doing I'd said, 'No.' Later on, I would think long and hard about why I'd said that and all I could come up with was that it made things easier to explain. No excuse, I know, but I'd said it and I was glad when she then started to tell me a bit about herself.

She was twenty three years old, which of course I already knew, and she had lived in the town all her life. She'd moved back in to live with her mum the previous year after her dad had died suddenly in a late-night car crash. 'I'll move out again,' she told me before she finished the dregs of her coffee, 'but I just needed to make sure that Mum was OK.'

'And is she?' I asked.

On reflection it was a stupid question, which Angela confirmed when she answered, 'As OK as she'll ever be.'

She looked off into a space behind my shoulder for a second and I guessed that she was thinking about her dad so I let her do that for as long as she wanted to.

'They were childhood sweethearts,' she told me, 'and neither of them ever had another partner. They were only nineteen when they got married and my eldest brother was born six month later.'

The maths wasn't lost on me but I didn't say anything.

By the time she left, just before two in the morning, we'd had two more mugs of coffee and I'd discovered that in addition to her eldest brother there were two more, both older, and a younger sister. I also knew that she preferred cats to dogs, apples to oranges, and that she'd tried vegetarianism for a week before the call of a bacon sandwich defeated her.

'Are you sure you don't want me to walk you home?' I asked as she threw her jacket over her head and slid it over her arms.

'Don't be daft,' she laughed. 'I'll be home in five minutes.'

I conceded and took her downstairs. I opened the back door and let her out and she laughed saying that she'd be home in four minutes now because she'd cut the corner off.

We stood in the doorway and she looked up into my face. Was I supposed to kiss her? I wanted to, but before I could make a move she made hers and pecked me on the cheek.

'Goodnight, Rob,' she said. 'See you tomorrow.'

''Night Angela,' I said.

She took a step or two and then she stopped and looked over her shoulder.

'Call me Angie,' she said before she disappeared into the darkness.

TOM

Two years later we had another portrait of our sons done except this time there were three of them. Michael had been born three months earlier.

Simon, who was almost six sat with the baby on his lap resting against his chest. Anthony sat to the side of them holding the baby's hand. All three of them smiled at the camera though, in all honesty, Michael's smile was probably down to wind rather than the faces that I was pulling from my position behind the photographer.

When we got the canvas back, we took a copy to Michelle's parents and then went to Mum and Dad's to drop one off for them.

'You've got three fine looking boys, Tom,' Dad said, in a matter of fact sort of way. He had replaced the original portrait above the fireplace with the new one and he was looking at it as he spoke. I looked at it too and I knew that he was speaking the truth. They were beautiful boys. They all had their father's blond hair and their mother's brown eyes.

Michael had been asleep on Michelle's lap but he started to stir. He opened his eyes briefly but it was like there was nothing to interest him going on so he closed them again. Anthony was on the floor building a tower with oversized building blocks and Simon was running a car along the arm of the chair that my mother was sitting in.

'Do you like cars, Simon?' my mum asked.

'Yes,' he replied without looking at her.

'Your daddy always liked cars,' she said and, as she brushed his fringe away from his eyes, I noticed a look on her face that was sort of far away, distant. Michelle didn't lift her eyes from Michael, and Dad was helping Anthony to balance the tower that was probably a couple of bricks too tall. Either I was the only one to hear what my mother had said or they were both making a point of ignoring it.

'Did you, Daddy? Did you like cars?' Simon's eyes were bright and there was an excitement in his voice.

I looked at Mum but she didn't look at me. I got the feeling that she was deliberately not meeting my gaze so I let it go and looked at Simon.

'Yes,' I said, 'I did always like cars, but I liked trains more.'

Mum looked up at me then, and I could tell that she was trying to say something with her eyes. The trouble was that I didn't know what it was but I doubted it was anything resembling an apology.

Michelle asked me about it later that evening. The boys had been in bed for a while and we were settled on the sofa. I was sitting on one end and Michelle had her feet up and her back to me as my arm rested over her shoulder. It was our default position for watching television.

When she started stroking my hand that was resting on her chest, I knew that there was something that she wanted to say. We'd been married long enough for me to know the signs.

'What happened earlier?' she asked. I asked her what she meant, though I thought I knew what she was referring to. She pushed herself up and swivelled on the seat so that she could see me. She looked me straight in the eye and asked, 'What happened at your mum's?'

I didn't bother pretending that I didn't know what she was talking about, but I did try to dismiss it and said, 'It was nothing.'

She did that thing where she raises one eyebrow as if to say *do I look stupid*? and I couldn't help laughing because I've asked her a thousand times how she does it. *She* didn't laugh though, and it was obvious there was no way I was getting out of telling her.

'She was confused, that was all.' I tried to make it sound insignificant.

'What about?' her eyebrow had dropped but she still looked sceptical.

'She told Simon that his daddy used to like cars,' I said.

'What's wrong with that?' It was a simple enough question and there was only one answer to it.

'It was Robert who liked cars.'

I knew that she was looking at me but I couldn't look at her – I focused on her knee... of all places! Out of the corner of my eye I saw her move her hand and then felt it on the side of my face. Her thumb stroked my ear. 'Like you said, she just got a bit confused.' She spoke softly, the way I'd heard her speak to the boys a thousand times before.

I tried to smile but it wasn't until she smiled at me that I managed it.

'You're right,' I admitted.

'If she needs us to remind her who Simon's father is,' she said as she settled back into position, resting on my chest, 'I can always take his birth certificate over for her to see.'

I kissed the top of her head but I wished that I could see her face.

The phone rang an hour or two later and I jumped up to answer it as quickly as I could. The last thing we needed was one of the boys waking up.

'Hello,' I said almost under my breath so that I didn't make too much noise. I was surprised when I heard my mother's voice and instantly wondered what the problem was. 'What's wrong?' I asked and I could hear the concern in my own voice.

'I want to see you,' she said.

'What about?'

I'd asked what I thought was a perfectly sensible question but Mum got a bit snappy and said, 'Does a mother need a reason to see her son?'

I heard her give a big sigh and then say, 'I just need to see you, Tom,' in a much calmer voice.

The fact that she said *need* the second time rather than *want* wasn't lost on me. I asked her if it would keep and when she said that it could I told her that I'd call round the following day after work.

'Who was that?' Michelle asked as she leaned forward

to allow me to get back into position.

'Mum,' I said simply.

'Everything all right?'

'Dunno,' I admitted as I settled back down. 'I'll find out tomorrow. I'm popping over after work.'

Michelle didn't speculate, at least out loud, about why Mum had called and asked to see me but I'm sure she did in her head and I'm sure that she reached the same conclusion that I had: that it had something to do with what had happened earlier that afternoon.

So the following evening, instead of going home after work, I went to my parents' house. Dad wasn't home yet but Mum was in the kitchen and she called for me to join her before I was even through the door. She asked me if I wanted a cup of tea and I nodded. I sat at the table and watched her as she went about the business of preparing the tea and, trust me, it was a bit of a performance. She had only given up using tea leaves a couple of years before but she still insisted on using a teapot even if she was only making one cup. She put some boiled water into the empty pot, swirled it round a bit and then emptied that water down the sink. Then the tea bags were dropped in the pot and the boiled water poured on top of them. Three minutes later she poured some tea into a china mug and added milk to it before passing it to me. She only ever uses china for tea. She reckons tea tastes better out of china but, to be honest, I've never noticed any difference. She poured herself a cup and then sat in the chair opposite me.

I watched her looking into her mug of tea for a few

seconds and then I asked, 'What's wrong?'

'Who said anything's wrong?' she asked, without raising her eyes.

I took a sip of tea and then reminded her that she'd asked to see me.

She took a couple of deep breaths and a sip of tea then made a heavy sigh before she said, 'I want to tell you something.'

'That sounds serious.' The thought that one of them was ill went through my mind.

Her mug was back on the table and she twisted it as she spoke. 'I wanted to say that I'm sorry,' she whispered.

I didn't need to ask her what she was sorry for but I did anyway.

'For yesterday.'

I knew I was being an arse but that didn't stop me asking, 'What about yesterday?' I just needed to hear her say it.

She looked uncomfortable as she said, 'When I told Simon that his daddy liked to play with cars.'

'I did like playing with cars,' I told her, 'I just liked playing with trains more.' Our eyes met and I vowed that I wasn't going to be the first to look away. I guess I wanted to prove a point.

She lowered her eyes and I think she nodded her head just a little bit. 'I should have known that,' she admitted.

Part of me wanted to say that she did know that but instead I said, 'You got confused, that's all.'

As I drove home I replayed the conversation in my

head. Mum was the only person who hadn't fully accepted that I was Simon's father. Even after all these years she hadn't come to terms with the situation. As usual, she said and did all the right things but, in her heart of hearts, I knew that she still thought of Simon as Robert's son despite what it said on his birth certificate. Her uncharacteristic slip the day before was her subconscious mind working when it shouldn't have been and I imagined that was what she was sorry for.

I didn't blame her, not really. I mean, I was angry with her for thinking the way that she did but, thinking as a father and not as her son, I could understand it. At the end of the day Robert was still her son and she would always love him. I would feel the same way about my sons – all three of them. What hurt me though was that I was her son too and, even after everything that had happened, I knew that she still loved Robert more.

It sounds stupid when I say it – I was a grown man after all – but it was just the way I felt.

ROBERT

Angie and I became what we used to call 'an item' and saw each other not only at work but also on our days off. Being the one who did the rotas for myself and the other three people that worked at the pub, I could have made sure that we were always off together, but I didn't do that. I knew that Danny and Colin were pretty laid back but I was sure even they had their limits, especially Colin. I'd seen him in a temper once and I wouldn't like to think that I might be on the wrong end of it. Plus, Angie and I weren't joined at the hip and I needed some time to myself even if she didn't.

Angie wasn't needy in the way that Diane had been. We would go out to the cinema or for a meal and from time to time she would spend the night, but she never left as much as a toothbrush in my flat.

One night, must have been around November I think, we went to a wedding at the Castle – a hotel overlooking the sea. We only went to the night reception but it was still a good do. You'd want it to be though, wouldn't you, if you paying what they were to hire that place? Even in the off season I bet it was costing an arm and a leg.

The beer wasn't much to write home about considering it was the best part of three quid a pint but, lucky for me, the bride's father was a generous man and spent most of the night propping up the bar dipping into his wallet. He

147

allowed me to buy him one drink later on but he must have bought us half a dozen or more. More probably, because I can take my drink, but by the time we walked home I was well and truly sozzled. Angie was staying at mine that night and once we were home we decided to have a night cap.

We went into the bar and, while Angie sat at the one table that the street light caught, I nipped behind the bar to get us a couple of drinks. I poured myself a whisky with a dash of water and got one of those Irish cream things for Angie. I scribbled an IOU on a beer mat, propped it up against the till and carried the drinks to where Angie was now tipping her chair so the back was against the wall behind her. She straightened up when I put the drink in front of her and after I'd sat down she held her glass up in a toast though she didn't say what she was toasting.

We both took a sip and Angie rested the back of her chair against the wall again. After a couple of minutes, she lifted the glass towards her lips and I noticed that she held it just short of her mouth. I looked at her and saw that she was looking at me.

'What's wrong?' I asked.

She answered with one word, 'You.'

'What about me?' I fortified myself with a sip of my own drink because I wasn't sure what was coming next.

'Why are you really here, Rob?' she asked.

Maybe it was… no, definitely it was the alcohol that loosened my tongue because I told her.

'Running away.'

It was too late, the words were out and, as my mum has said many a time, once something has been said, there's no unsaying it.

Angie took another sip of her drink, throwing her head back as she swallowed. When she lowered her head, she looked me straight in the eye and said, 'Knew it.'

Had she? How could she? I was about to ask her but I didn't get chance because she had another question.

'What are you running away from?'

I'm pretty sure that even in my drink-muddled state I could have made something up, but I didn't. 'From a girl,' I said.

She nodded slowly and said, 'OK,' as she screwed her lips together and leaned forward so her chair wasn't tipping backwards anymore.

She didn't ask me to but I told her anyway and once I started talking the words just poured out of me.

'My girlfriend got pregnant.' I said the words slowly. 'I wasn't ready to be a parent. I think if I'd have stayed Michelle would have wanted to get married and I definitely wasn't ready to be a husband.' After a large gulp of whisky, I told her how I'd made the decision to do a runner and left without actually facing anyone. I told her about the letters that I'd left and what I'd written in them. I told her everything, and then I tossed what was left in my glass down my neck and said I was getting another. Angie held her glass up to show that she'd have a refill too and I noticed that she smiled at me.

As I poured the drinks I realised that I didn't feel drunk

anymore. I still took my time walking back to the table, not because I was unsteady, but because I didn't know what Angie was going to say next – or if I wanted to hear it.

She didn't say anything for a few seconds, which felt more like hours. I don't like being judged for what I do but I knew that what Angie thought mattered to me.

'Have you had nothing to do with them since you left?' she asked, sounding sceptical, like she found it hard to believe that what I was saying could be true even though I'd assured her that it was.

'What about the CSA?' she asked.

I didn't understand what she meant. Sorry, I don't really keep up with current affairs or whatever they call them, so I didn't know what she was talking about. She explained who they were and what they did.

'A friend of mine went to them so that she could get money from her baby's dad,' she told me, and she laughed when I reminded her that Michelle didn't know where I was. 'No, sweetheart,' she laughed, 'but I'm sure the authorities could track you down.' The fact that she called me sweetheart took me by surprise, even though she'd said it in a jokey way, and I didn't know what to say. So Angie kept talking. 'Which means that she probably didn't keep the baby.'

'What?' I thought I hadn't heard her properly.

'Think about it,' she said. 'If... Michelle was it?' I nodded. 'If Michelle had kept the baby, the CSA would have been on to you for child support. I'm guessing that you paid tax in your old job and you pay tax here, so it would have been a doddle for them to find you.'

It made sense, I suppose, but I still struggled with the idea that Michelle hadn't kept the baby. What had she done with it? She wouldn't have got rid of it and I really couldn't imagine her giving it up for adoption. That only left one thing. She must have lost it. Yes, I decided. That was it. Michelle had had a miscarriage.

Maybe it had been for the best.

Later on, after Angie and I had made love and she was lying beside me resting her head on my chest, I thought of Michelle and how it used to feel to have her lying in my arms. I wondered how she was now. How she was coping.

I was sure that Angie was right about the baby, about there not being one, or – at least – not one that Michelle was taking care of. Not one that I was responsible for anyway.

I know this probably sounds ridiculous but I felt sad. Not for me, because I'd not wanted anything to do with a baby, but for Michelle. She'd have made a great mum. I knew that she would have taken a miscarriage badly and I hoped that she was over it.

In the morning I woke to the sound of rattling cups in the kitchen and a couple of minutes later Angie appeared carrying two mugs of coffee. She was wearing the T-shirt that I had thrown on the back of a chair the night before and it did little to cover her modesty, not that she had much to cover. I sat up and she climbed in beside me. She asked me if I was all right and smiled as she handed me my cup.

She didn't mention what we had spoken about the night before. In fact, she never did.

Angie moved in with me shortly after that and I was happy, really happy, for the first time in ages.

TOM

The boys looked at their new cousin with varying degrees of interest.

Michael stood on tiptoe to try and see into the Moses basket to find out what all the fuss was about. Anthony held his finger within the baby's reach and smiled when it was grabbed, while Simon's eyes flicked from the baby to her parents and then back at the baby. He was a bright boy and the last time he had seen his Auntie Jane she'd had a big stomach. Now her stomach was much flatter and there was a baby. I thought he'd probably worked out that the two things were connected and fully expected to have an interesting conversation with him later.

'Where did baby Emily come from?' he asked, not long after we got home.

We'd talked about how we would approach this subject when it was brought up so I said, 'From Auntie Jane's tummy,' in as matter of fact a tone as I could manage.

'How did she get there?' He didn't look up from the toy farm that he was playing with.

'Uncle Craig put her there,' Michelle said in the same tone as I had used.

He stopped what he was doing and chewed his lip then he looked at his mum and asked, 'Did I come from your tummy?'

'Yes, you did,' she said it softly and smiled.

'And did Daddy put me there?' He made it sound like a ridiculous idea.

Michelle stretched her arm out so that she could stroke his head, 'Well you didn't get there by yourself did you,' she said.

He went back to placing the cows in a circle and the conversation seemed to be over. Michelle and I shared a smile and a sigh of relief.

We didn't consciously hide Robert's existence from our sons. We had mentioned Uncle Robert in passing, you know things like 'Daddy and Uncle Robert did this or that,' but we'd never really been sure if anything had registered. Apparently enough had because, one day not long after his seventh birthday Simon asked, 'Why don't we see Uncle Robert?'

We were sitting at the kitchen table when he asked the question. Michelle was serving up the Sunday lunch and I can still see her as she stopped mid-action with a spoonful of mashed potato halfway between the saucepan and a plate. I could see her hand shaking and that familiar look of fear in her eyes.

'He doesn't live here,' I said as I poured some orange juice into the beaker that Simon was holding.

'Where does he live?' he lifted the beaker to his mouth and slurped loudly. I told him that I didn't know and hoped that would be the end of it, but it wasn't. Simon had another question, 'Doesn't Gran know where he lives?'

'I don't know,' I said, grateful that Michelle put his

food in front of him at that point. Simon's stomach always came first and the conversation was finished, though I suspected only temporarily.

A couple of nights later, when the boys were tucked up in bed, I sat on the sofa with the newspaper open on my lap. I doubt I was reading it because I rarely do. I tend to just flick through. Anyway, that's what I was doing when Michelle came into the room carrying Simon's drawing pad. She opened it up and handed it to me.

I looked at the picture and asked, 'What's this?'

'Something Simon drew today,' she said as she sat on the other end of the sofa and watched for my reaction.

I saw a collection of people of different shapes and sizes and I realised that they were a family. It was our family. Michelle and I were there holding hands with each other and there were three children standing in front of us. There wasn't a lot of difference in size between the boys but we could identify them by the fact that for some reason they were each wearing their favourite hat. There were two sets of grandparents at one side and at the other side was Craig with Jane who was holding a ball that I assumed was baby Emily.

I didn't notice at first, but Simon had drawn another figure. It was alone and smaller than the rest which made it look like it was standing in the background.

'Who's that?' I asked.

Michelle's voice cracked as she told me. 'Uncle Robert.'

We'd made a conscious decision not to hide the fact that I had a brother, and now Simon was taking an interest in him. We only had ourselves to blame really, but what choice had we had? I did have a brother.

Simon had drawn his mythical uncle off to the side of the family group, there but not quite part of it. On the outside.

We spent the next nine years hoping it would stay that way.

ROBERT

Angie and I were good together. We were good for each other. She knew all about my past and over the next few years she told me about hers – and neither of us judged the other person. We made a good team. So much so that when Phil died and Gloria decided to sell The Brown Bull, Angie and I bought it. Well, I'd been running it for years and, as Gloria said, it was practically mine anyway.

She gave us a good price – too good a price if I'm honest – but the place held too many memories for her and I think she just wanted rid of it. I had to come up with a business plan for the bank of course, but that was a piece of piss because during the time that I had been managing The Bull, turnover had increased and profits were up.

So, there I was, thirty-two years old with a business of my own. As a young lad I'd dreamt of being my own boss, though I'd never seen myself as a pub landlord. Do you know what, though? I couldn't get the smile off my face the day my name went above the door.

That day was in August so the place had been bouncing with holiday makers as well as the loyal locals that saw us through the off-season. Like some sort of madman I offered everybody a drink on the house.

'You'll not make a profit that way,' Angie teased as we passed each other on our way to different ends of the bar and I smiled at her.

'*We'll* not make a profit,' I corrected, 'and if it bothers you that much you can take it out of my hide later.'

She smiled at that but I don't know if it was the reminder that we were in this together or the prospect of rampant sex that caused it.

There was no sex, rampant or otherwise, that night because by the time we'd sent the last punter on his way and locked the door behind him we were knackered. When we got up to the flat all either of us was good for was sitting on the sofa with a cup of tea while we unwound. That's the thing about finishing work at midnight, you can't just go to bed and fall asleep, you need to take some time to unwind and, I've got to tell you, I was so wound up that night I wasn't sure I'd get any sleep at all. I know that the pub had officially been mine – sorry *ours* – for a few weeks but that was the first night that my name, *my* name, had been over the door and my head was buzzing. I was so excited.

Even with the drinks that we had given away we would still make a profit, and I couldn't help feeling that this was the start of something. I know it sounds corny, but you find yourself in the position I was in and tell me you wouldn't have felt the same.

'You're quiet,' Angie said after a while.

Was I? I hadn't realised it but I guessed she was right because a lot of things were going through my head.

'You all right?'

'Never better,' I said as I rested my arm across the back of the sofa as an invitation for her to come closer if she wanted to. 'I was just thinking.'

She shuffled along, settled in beside me and asked, 'What were you thinking about?'

'This and that,' I said vaguely, not wanting to tell her what had really been on my mind just before she asked the question.

The trouble is that in our years together Angie had learned how to read the signs and probably knew me better than I knew myself. She hit the nail on the head when she said, 'You were thinking about home weren't you? You were thinking about your family.'

I put the mug I'd been resting on my knee onto the table at the side of the sofa, freeing up my other arm so that I could wrap both of them around her. 'This is home,' I said.

'You know what I mean, you were thinking about the home you had before this.' Of course I'd known what she meant, I'd just hoped that if I made light of it she would let it go.

I should have known better. Once I'd accepted she wasn't going to drop it, I thought we might as well have the conversation so I said, 'Not the place really, more the people.'

She didn't say anything, but her silence was just another way of her asking me to keep talking.

'I was just wondering what they'd think, you know, Mum and Dad and our Tom. What would they think about me owning a pub? They'd never imagine it in a million years. My own garage one day if I'd won the lottery, but not a pub.'

'I'd bet they'd be proud of you.'

The words were muffled into my chest but I'm sure that's what she said.

Would they be? I thought about that one for a few seconds before I answered. 'Maybe.'

Before I had a chance to give it any more thought Angie had bounced off the sofa and onto my knee. She straddled me so that she was facing me.

'Maybe?' she said. 'Why "maybe"? Of course they'd be proud of you.'

'I know. But they'd have been really hurt when I left, especially the way I left…'

'But that was ages ago,' she said. 'Things change, people change.' She held my head in her hands and her face was just inches from mine. 'You've done something good with your life. Of course they'd be proud.'

'I know, but…' she cut me off before I could finish the sentence.

'Look,' she said, 'I know it wasn't your finest hour but you did what you thought you had to do, what was best for you.' She paused just long enough to draw breath. 'You're not the person you were back then, you've moved on. They'll have moved on too.'

She paused longer this time and then hit me with a bombshell. 'Maybe now is the time to get back in touch with them.'

The thought of it brought me out in a cold sweat but I told her I'd think about it. I was surprised when she left it at that but I knew she would bring it up again some time.

Long after Angie was asleep beside me, and even though I was completely exhausted, I lay awake thinking about what I'd once had. I'm not especially talking about Michelle. It was more my parents and my brother that filled my thoughts.

When I'd left Tom was a slightly drippy art student. No, that's not fair. He wasn't drippy, he just wasn't like me. He preferred using his brain to his hands and, while I was mortal drunk most Saturday nights, I never saw him even tipsy. To look at, we were almost the same but in all other ways we were chalk and cheese.

I wondered what he was up to. He'd have been thirty by then and I imagined him settled down with a girl he'd met at college, a fellow art student maybe. They'd be living in some Bohemian heaven where she made bread and they ate lentils with everything. I couldn't help smiling at that, though I knew I was being cruel. Tom was a good kid. I hoped he'd done well for himself.

When I thought about my parents, even though I knew it was ridiculous, I saw them as they had been: I saw Mum, as she was that last morning when she told me she'd heard me moving around during the night and banged on about me not having breakfast. I couldn't imagine her having changed much in the intervening years. She'd been almost fifty when I left so she must be nearly sixty by now. As for Dad, he'd already be sixty. He'd had a big birthday and I'd missed it. I wondered what else I'd missed.

I know that the thought should have occurred to me then but it didn't and wouldn't for a few more years. What if I had missed something more important than a big birthday? What if I'd missed something like a funeral? When I did think about it, I would decide that surely I would know if one of them had died, I would *feel* it – and I would quickly dismiss the thought.

Back when Angie suggested it I just decided that 'now' wasn't the right time. I would get in touch again but only when the time was right. It would be a good few years before the time turned out to be right.

I surprised the hell out of Angie by telling her what I was going to do and she asked the obvious question.

'Why now?'

I couldn't answer her because I didn't really know the reason. I just knew that the thought had come to me a few weeks earlier and wouldn't go away. It kept coming back to me, especially in the dark hours of the early morning, and that morning I'd decided it was what I wanted to do. I tried explaining it to Angie, but I didn't expect her to understand. How could she when even I didn't?

She said that if it was what I thought, then I should do it; and I should do it before I changed my mind. 'Trust your instinct Rob,' she told me.

'But it's been over sixteen years,' I said.

'That doesn't matter,' Angie said, realising that I was already starting to talk myself out of it. 'They're your family.'

'They might not want to see me,' I said, feeling pathetic. That was my biggest fear.

'Then you'll come back here, we'll get raging drunk, and we'll carry on as we have been.'

She made it sound so simple.

I set off that afternoon.

TOM

Just after the Christmas following Simon's sixteenth birthday my dad started to have some health problems. At first it was nothing specific, just a cold that lingered, but as time went by it developed into a chest infection. After that had cleared up he was left with underlying lung issues that the doctors couldn't seem to pin down. I know it sounds daft but, for the first time, we became aware of the fact that our parents wouldn't live for ever and we made a conscious effort to visit them more often. I popped in to see my mum and dad at least twice a week after work and Michelle did the same with hers.

By the summer, the visits had become a regular part of our lives.

I didn't pay close attention to the unfamiliar car that was parked a little further along the street – I noticed that it was green and thought it looked like a Fiesta, but I couldn't be sure. I could see the silhouette of someone in the driver's seat so I guessed that they were either coming or going and I didn't really care which.

When I left an hour or so later, I gave a cursory glance up and down the street to check for oncoming traffic before I opened the driver's door of my car. I wasn't surprised to see the green car still parked where it had been until I noticed there was still someone sitting in the driver's seat. I wondered what were the chances of them arriving and leaving at the same time as I had; what a coincidence.

I got in the car, settled into the seat, started the engine and made a mental note to ask my mum about the people that had moved into the house that the green car was parked in front of. I assumed it had finally been sold and I was curious about who had moved into the house that my friend Paul had lived in. I put the car in gear and had to wait for a red Mini to pass before I could move off.

As I pulled alongside the green car, which *was* a Fiesta, by the way, the man in the driver's seat turned away as if looking at something on the passenger seat. Trouble for him was that he hadn't turned far enough. My stomach lurched when I saw the familiar tilt to the stranger's head.

When I got home, the talk was of Simon's impending GCSE results and the need to get Michael another pair of regulation charcoal grey trousers before he started secondary school in a few weeks' time.

The boys in question both took my arrival as an excuse to leave the room and Michelle told them not to go far as tea wouldn't be long. She smiled at me and mouthed a greeting in my direction. I forced a smile, but I couldn't fool my wife.

'You all right?' she asked.

I said that I was but she wasn't convinced and asked if I was sure.

'Yeah,' I nodded my head to emphasise my answer but I didn't meet her eyes.

'How's your dad?' she asked as she turned her attention back to what she was cooking.

'He's good,' I said. 'Mum says he hasn't coughed all day.' I'd moved across the kitchen to stand beside her and I rested my hip on the counter as I looked at her. I wanted to tell her what I thought I'd seen but I didn't have the words and, when she smiled at me again, I didn't have the heart to say anything. Instead I said, 'Have I got time to get changed?' and she said that tea would be about ten minutes. I used that as a chance to go to our bedroom.

Once there I closed the door, turned around, and rested my weight against it. I let my head fall backwards and my eyes settled on the place where the wall met the ceiling. I could feel my heart pounding in my chest and I was taking short sharp breaths. For the first time in my life I had a panic attack.

I knew what – or rather who – I had seen and no matter how much I wanted to be wrong I knew that I wasn't.

I would have known him anywhere.

The first thing I noticed when I visited my parents a couple of nights later was that there was no sign of the green Fiesta or its occupant. The second thing that I noticed was that Dad was in the garden.

'What you up to?' I asked. 'I thought the doctor told you to take it easy.'

He leaned on his spade and said, 'I am.' He took a sneaky look at the house and said, 'I've had to come out here. Your mum's driving me nuts.'

'Why?' I asked. 'What's wrong with her?'

'You tell me!' Dad dabbed the ground with a spade but didn't make a dent in the soil that hadn't been rained on for days. 'She can't sit still for two minutes,' he said. 'Up and down, up and down, all day long.'

'Oh?' I looked over Dad's shoulder and caught a glimpse of Mum at the window of what used to be my bedroom. She quickly moved behind the curtain when she realised that I'd seen her. Before she noticed me, she had been looking further up the street and I knew that she had been looking at where the green Fiesta had been parked.

'She just can't settle,' Dad said. 'She's been like this for a week or more.'

Later, I lay in bed and listened to the rhythmic sound of Michelle's breathing. It was a noise that I had come to love over the years and it had always brought me comfort. But that night it did nothing to calm me. From what I'd seen and what my dad had told me I realised my mother knew what I knew. And I no good could come of it. I doubted she felt the same.

It was a long time before I finally fell asleep but, when I did, I dreamt of green Fiestas, a familiar face, and my world crashing down around my ears.

'Are you sure everything is all right?' Michelle asked over the breakfast table the following morning. 'You tossed and turned a lot last night.'

'I'm sorry,' I said without answering her question. 'I didn't mean to disturb you.'

She was going through the morning rituals and, as I watched her clearing plates and putting them in the sink, I toyed with the idea of telling her what I'd seen. But I asked myself what it was that I actually *knew*: I didn't really know anything, not for sure.

All right, I did know something, I suppose, but nothing would be gained by telling her, not then anyway. I convinced myself there would be plenty of time for that. But the truth was that there might not be: I knew my brother and I knew that Robert would do whatever he thought was best for Robert. If that meant turning up on the doorstep without warning, he would think nothing of it. I'd have to prepare Michelle, and soon. I just didn't know how.

For as long as I can remember my mother has done her grocery shopping on a Friday morning. The following Thursday afternoon I saw my boss and told him that I was going to need a couple of hours off the next day.

'Everything OK, Tom?' he asked. 'Is your dad all right?'

I assured him that Dad was fine and thanked him for asking. I told him that there was just something that I needed to do. I'd developed a good relationship with him over the years and he knew I wouldn't ask if it wasn't important. He said to let him know if there was anything he could do.

Dad was surprised when I walked through the door the following morning about half nine. He'd been in the living room when I went through the door and shouted that it was only me. He appeared in the doorway and asked, 'What are you doing here?'

'Charming,' I said, trying to sound light hearted. 'Just thought I'd pop in for a brew.'

A few minutes later I carried two mugs of tea into the living room and placed one on the coffee table in front of my dad while I sat opposite cradling my own cup in my hands.

We sat in silence for a minute or two and then Dad asked, 'What's bothering you, son?'

I looked at him and didn't know where to start. I took a sip of the tea just to give myself some thinking time. Dad watched me and waited and eventually I knew I was going to have to tell him what was on my mind.

'Robert's back.' I spat the words out as quickly as I could.

He had been about to take a sip of his own drink and the mug had been halfway to his mouth when I spoke. It stayed there as what I said registered and then he slowly lowered the mug and put it back on the table. He looked at me and asked, 'What did you say?'

I put my mug down on the table too because my hands were shaking and I didn't trust myself not to spill it. I looked at him for a second or two before I told him about what I'd seen.

'I saw him across the road,' I said.

Dad shuffled forward in his seat but didn't say anything. He just cocked his head to one side and waited for me to explain.

'I noticed someone sitting in a green car across the road the other day. I just assumed that someone had finally moved into number six and didn't give it much thought then, but they were still there sitting in the car when I left.' I could hear a tremor in my voice as I said, 'When I drove past I looked across and they looked away, pretending to look at something on the passenger seat.'

'And you think it was Robert?' Dad sounded sceptical – or was it hopeful? It was hard to tell.

'I'm sure it was Robert,' I insisted.

'But you said he turned away.' I don't think Dad wanted to believe it any more than I did.

'Not far enough,' I said. Now that the words were out I relaxed and I took a huge mouthful of tea, enjoying the sensation of swallowing it even though it was still way too hot.

'It's been sixteen years,' he said. 'Are you sure?'

'Positive.' As I spoke, I noticed his face losing colour.

He put his hand on top of his head and pushed the little hair he had left as far back as it would go. 'Oh my God,' he said slowly.

'I think Mum knows,' I told him and, once he'd digested that, he started to nod his head again. His face changed as disbelief was replaced by acceptance and I could almost see the pieces falling into place.

We sat in silence together, united in the knowledge that the lives we had lived for over a decade and a half were about to change. And I'm sure that Dad knew as well as I did that it was unlikely that the change would be for the better.

I leaned forward looking at the floor between my feet and Dad lay back, resting his head on the back of the chair. His head was turned to the window like he was looking through it but I'm not sure he was.

I don't know how it happened but we sat there much longer than I had planned. The next thing I knew Mum was doing what I had done, and the front door closed seconds after we heard her shout, 'It's only me.'

Dad turned his head and looked towards the door, waiting for her to appear. 'Are you in here, Bob?' She popped her head into the room and was obviously surprised to me. 'What are you doing here, Tom?' she asked. 'What's wrong?'

'Why would anything be wrong?'

She looked uncomfortable as I locked eyes with her.

'There's nothing wrong with Michelle and the boys is there?'

'No,' I said slowly without taking my eyes off her. 'They're fine.'

A look of panic spread quickly over her face and that was all the confirmation that we needed. She almost fell into a chair. Dad and I looked at her but she was looking off to the side.

'How long have you known love?' Dad asked tenderly.

'Known what?' She tried to sound as though she had no idea what we were talking about, but she fooled no one.

'That he's back,' Dad prompted.

'Back?' she said. 'Who's back? Back from where?' Her

voice was high pitched and a bit squeaky, a sure sign that she knew exactly what Dad was talking about.

'*Him!*' I said the word like an obscenity.

'Him who?'

I couldn't help feeling that the way she was trying to keep up the pretence was pathetic.

Dad put a stop to it, telling her, 'Tom's seen him too.'

She dropped her eyes for a second or two and when she lifted them up I thought there was something like joy in her eyes. She looked at me and asked, 'Are you sure it's him?'

'Aren't you?'

She sucked a deep breath in and couldn't help a small smile forming across her lips. 'I'd know him anywhere,' she said.

As I buried my head in my hands I heard Dad ask, 'When did he come back?'

She didn't speak straight away and I raised my head to see what she was doing. It seemed to me as though she was collecting her thoughts because her eyes were flicking around. It was like she was trying to put things in some sort of order. She spoke slowly.

'About three weeks ago. I was coming home from the doctors when I saw him in the park standing on the stone bridge. Then a few days later I saw a green car up the street and he was sitting in it. I've seen him there a few more times since then.'

'Have you spoken to him?' Dad asked the question before I could,

'No,' she said quickly and this time I thought she was

telling the truth.

Then Dad asked, 'Has he been to this house?' which was the other question I'd wanted to ask.

'No,' she said 'I thought he would, but so far he hasn't.' I wanted to believe she wasn't lying that time too.

'What does he want?' Dad was just thinking out loud but I answered him anyway.

'He wants whatever is best for him,' I said. I felt Mum looking at me and when I looked at her I saw pain in her eyes but I didn't care. 'Oh, come on, Mum.' I said harshly. 'Let's not pretend there'd be any other reason.'

'Maybe he's sorry,' she said pitifully.

'It's too late for sorry,' I said as I pushed myself out of the chair, 'nearly seventeen years too late.'

'Where are you going?' She stretched her hand out but I pulled my arm out of her reach.

'Work,' I said and after a nod towards my dad I left the house as quickly as I could.

I sat in the car and looked at the space where the green car had been parked. I didn't need to look to know that I was being watched through a window. I started the car and drove away slowly.

When I got to work, Derek, my boss, showed some concern and asked again if I was all right. I told him I was but I don't think he believed me and he left me alone for the rest of the day. I spent the afternoon going through the motions, and by the time I left I had achieved absolutely nothing of any consequence.

I drove the long way home and tried to get my thoughts

into some sort of order, but failed miserably. I went into the house with the intention of appearing as normal as possible. The boys were watching TV in the living room and I asked where their mother was. Michael said that she was upstairs.

When I walked into the bedroom Michelle was getting changed into clothes she could relax in. She had returned to nursing about six or seven years earlier and worked on the surgical ward at the General Hospital. She had finished her shift at about four and would have picked the younger boys up from her mother's on her way home.

I smiled at her and set about getting changed myself, happy to be taking off the shirt and tie that I had worn all day.

'Your mum rang,' she said as she slipped out of her dress.

'When?' I know I was sharp because Michelle moved her head back as if she'd been slapped.

'About ten minutes ago,' she said, taken aback. 'I hadn't long got back from Mum's.'

I took a deep breath and asked, 'What did she want?'

Michelle put the uniform dress on a hanger and told me, 'She just asked if you were home yet.'

'Why?' I tried to make it sound like I wasn't really interested.

'She didn't say,' Michelle pulled a T-shirt over her head as she spoke. When her head popped out of the top she smiled at me.

I smiled back at her. No matter what was going on, Michelle's smile could always make me feel better. I loved her more than I'd ever thought it was possible to love anyone and knew that I would do whatever I had to do to keep her.

I had the exact same thought again later on looking at the boys as we sat round the table sharing a meal and talking. This was the family time that I treasured the most. I knew that Robert wouldn't be interested in Anthony or Michael so they were safe from his clutches, but what about Simon? Would he be interested in Simon? Did he even know that Simon existed? Did he know that Michelle and I were married? Would he even care about that?

I asked myself what Robert would do but it was a question I couldn't answer. I've told you already that we had once been close, but even back then I wouldn't have liked to say with any certainty that I ever knew what Robert was thinking. And if I hadn't known then, what chance did I have now?

There were so many questions running through my head and I knew that there was only one person that could answer them. I just had to find him first.

ROBERT

I reversed the route that I had taken all those years before and was back in my home town less than two hours later. I'd spent the journey thinking about what I would do when I arrived but by the time I got there I was still no further forward.

The car was on autopilot really and, without realising that I'd been heading there, I found myself outside the garage that I had once worked in. Or at least I thought I was outside it: the school was still there at the end of the street, and the church was in front of me, but when I got out of the car and looked there was an estate agent's where the forecourt used to be and a solicitor's where the workshop once stood. I even checked the street sign to make sure I hadn't lost my bearings, and that confirmed that I was where I should be. It was the garage that wasn't.

As I drove along the street my primary school had been on, I found it was gone too, replaced by a series of the little boxes that laughingly passed for houses these days: new-builds with small rooms, tiny gardens and huge price tags.

That was the point that I really started to understand how much had changed in the years since I'd been gone, and as I drove past what had been my home, my heart sank. I searched for Dad's car and it wasn't there. I kicked myself for thinking it should have been; how could I be so stupid? The car had been about eight years old when I left, so of course it wouldn't be there. But shouldn't there be a car of some description? I couldn't imagine Dad not driving and surely his car would be there because it was about seven o'clock and way past the time he'd be home from work.

The rational part of me thought that maybe they had moved house, but they had lived there since the day they were married so I thought that was unlikely. I concluded that it could only mean one thing: Dad was dead. I was too late.

That was when I reminded myself of the belief that I would have felt... I don't know... *something* if one of them had died. Dad wasn't dead, there had to be another explanation. I told myself I was being overly dramatic.

I'd anticipated not being home that night so I had booked a hotel room over the phone. I drove to the hotel and checked in, then called Angie from my room.

'How'd it go?' she asked cheerily.

I had a one-word answer. 'Shite.'

She asked me what had happened.

'Everything's different,' I said, and even as the words came out I realised how stupid I must seem to have thought that things would be just as I had left them.

There was a silence, which Angie broke by asking, 'Did you see your parents?'

'No,' I admitted.

After we'd finished talking I went to the hotel bar and ordered a drink. When my beer came I cast a critical eye over it but decided what the hell and drank it anyway. Six pints later I climbed the stairs and let myself into the empty room. This was not how I'd seen the day ending. Maybe I'd been naïve to think that I'd spend the evening with Mum making a fuss of me as I told Dad about Angie and the pub. In my mind's eye, I'd even seen Tom rushing over from wherever the hell he lived now just so that he could shake my hand and say it was good to see me.

As I lay on my back staring at the ceiling I decided that maybe it was just as well I hadn't seen them because I was kidding myself about the reception that I would have received. Would they really have been so forgiving? I doubted that I would have been if I were in their shoes.

I slept fitfully and woke up tired. I'd promised Angie I would go back to the house, but I couldn't do it on an empty stomach so went down to the hotel restaurant. I asked the waitress for a Full English with white toast on the side and she brought me a cup of coffee while I waited. I took my time over the food, putting off what I knew I would have to do, so it was just before ten when I checked out. I'd only booked for one night so, come what may, I'd be going back to Angie before the day was out. At least I had something to look forward to.

The trouble was I had promised Angie I would try again. I just wasn't sure that I could, and in the end I didn't go to the house, I went to the park down the street. I watched the kids playing there, enjoying their summer holidays off school. The weather was good and most of them wore T-shirts and shorts. It occurred to me that I might look like some sort of weirdo eyeing up children so I walked away before someone called the police.

I walked up to where the café used to be, down past the tennis courts, and stopped on the stone bridge. I leaned against it and looked at the water running under it. I say running but it was standing really because the bridge was over a pond not a river.

After a while something made me look up and there she was: at a distance but it was definitely her. I put my head down so that she couldn't see my face but I didn't take my eyes off her. I watched her walk out of the park before I moved to a place where I could see where she was going.

She walked into the house. Mum still lived there, at least. I thought about going and knocking on the door but my feet wouldn't take me. They took me back to the car instead and I got in and drove home.

Angie didn't say that she was disappointed by what had happened, but I think she was. I knew *I* was. What the hell was wrong with me? She was my mother not the devil. She would have welcomed me back into the fold even if no one else did. I justified it by telling myself it was the lack of a car that threw me. A car, any car, would have suggested that Dad was still there with her. I couldn't get the thought that Dad might be dead out of my mind.

I told Angie how I felt.

'At least you would know,' she stroked my hair as she was talking to me, the way that a mother does when she's comforting her child.

The trouble was, I didn't think I was ready to know. Not if it turned out that I was right.

179

I went back the following week and I parked outside number six which was about a hundred yards up the street from my parents' house and on the other side. One of Tom's mates had lived there when we were little but the place looked like it was empty now. I had a good view of the front door.

It was a midweek afternoon and there was no sign of life in the house. In fact, there was no sign of life in the street. I sat there about twenty minutes, then left. I'd been in two minds about going that day because we had a function on at the pub that night and, although Angie had said they could manage without me, I used it as an excuse to get home as soon as I could.

'There was no one in,' I told Angie when she asked me what the hell I was doing back.

I'm not sure she believed me but she said she was glad I was there. 'It might get rowdy later on,' she said, 'and I think Colin's bouncing days might be behind him.'

I couldn't help feeling that I had let her down in some way.

By the time that I drove back to my home town the following week, it was as though the car knew its own way and when I parked up in the same spot as the week before there were several landmarks that I couldn't remember having passed. There had been an accident and I'd arrived later than I'd anticipated. It was after five and I thought I might have to stay over, depending on how things turned out.

I'd been there a couple of minutes plucking up the

courage to go up to the door and knock on it when a car appeared at the other end of the street. I watched a dark blue Vauxhall slow down and pull up outside the house. I got this feeling in the pit of my stomach which made me think of a washing machine on a fast spin as I wondered if I'd been proven wrong about Dad. I watched and waited to see if Dad got out of the car.

Dad didn't get out of the car. It was Tom, who gave a cursory glance in my direction before going up the path and walking straight into the house. No knocking for him. It occurred to me that maybe he still lived there.

I wanted to go up to the door, so help me God I did, but something stopped me. I was still sitting there when Tom came back out of the house. He looked in my direction again and I watched him looking at me. Do you know what surprised me the most about him? The way he was dressed. He was wearing light grey trousers and a charcoal jacket, with a tie hanging loosely around his neck. What had happened to my artistic younger brother? He looked like he worked in a bank. I wondered what had made Tom sell out on his dream.

He was still looking at me as he got back into his car. Then he pulled away slowly and, as he came closer, I turned my head away, pretending to look at something on the passenger seat.

Once he was past I looked in the rear-view mirror and watched him disappear around the corner and drive off in the direction of the ring road. I hadn't realised that I was holding my breath but I had been and I didn't let it go until

Tom was out of sight.

I sat a minute or two more then drove off. I was back behind the bar well before closing time.

After we'd cleared away and everyone else had left, Angie and I sat in the flat eating toast and drinking tea. What can I tell you? Being a pub landlord means you don't have a great diet. I think Angie had been waiting for me to tell her what had happened but when she thought she had waited long enough she asked.

'I saw Tom,' I told her.

She tried to appear casual as she asked, 'Did you speak to him?' But she didn't pull it off; she couldn't hide the excitement in her eyes.

That soon disappeared when I said, 'No.' I told her how I had seen him from my car, how I had watched him go into our parents' house and how I'd still been there when he left. 'Next time,' I told her. 'I promise Angie, next time I'll do it. I'll go up to the door and I'll knock on it.'

'When you're ready,' she said.

I still didn't know when that would be.

TOM

We both looked at the clock when the phone rang. Michelle was closest to it and said, 'Hello,' cautiously into the receiver. She nodded her head and flicked her eyes towards me as she said, 'OK.' She handed the phone to me and said, 'It's your dad,'

'Dad?' It was unusual for Dad to ring at all, let alone so late in the evening, so I was anxious to hear what he wanted. My first thought was that there was something wrong with Mum. I'm sorry, but when your parents reach a certain age the thought is always there at the back of your mind.

I thought I heard him say, 'He's here,' but not wanting to believe it I asked him to say it again. He did.

'He's here.'

I felt my heart pounding in my chest and I had to take a deep breath before I could ask, 'Where?'

'Sitting over the road, watching the house.'

I'd never heard my father sound so stressed in his life.

'I'm coming over,' I told him and handed the receiver back to Michelle without saying goodbye to my dad. 'I've got to go to Mum's,' I said on my way out of the room.

Michelle was on my heels asking, 'What's wrong? Is it your Mum? Do you want me to come with you?'

God no, I thought. That was the last thing I wanted. 'You stay here with the boys,' I said as I threw on a jacket and collected the car keys from the table in the hallway. 'I'll not be long.'

'But what's wrong?' she was like a dog with a bone sometimes. She reminds me of my dad in that respect.

'Nothing. Really.' I tried to make it sound frivolous but I was wasting my time.

'Why are you lying to me Tom?' she said directly into my eyes.

'Sorry,' I said after I'd blown air out of my cheeks. 'What I should have said was that it was nothing for you to worry about.'

She got that look on her face then, you know, the one that challenges you and I wilted under her glare. I probably did that childlike thing of chewing my lip as I considered my options and wondered how I was going to tell her. In the end I decided that the only thing to do was say it straight out. Like I'd done with my dad I spat the words 'Robert's back' out as quickly as I could.

'What?' Michelle whispered but it felt like she was screaming.

I reached out to her but for the first time ever she brushed my hand away. Her eyes were wide and wild and her mouth was moving without making a sound. She was taking short sharp breaths and it was a couple of seconds before she was controlled enough to ask, 'What do you mean?'

I think she hoped that she'd got the wrong end of the stick but when I said, 'He's turned up,' she realised she hadn't and she started to wobble. She let me grab her and I pulled her close.

'Where is he?' her voice wobbled almost as much as her legs had.

'At Mum's,' I said the words into the top of her head.

'At the house?' her voice was hysterical and her body stiffened.

'No,' I was still talking into the top of her head. 'He's sitting in a car across the street watching the house.'

She pulled away so that we were looking at each other. 'How do they know it's him, then?' hysteria had been replaced by desperation.

I had no choice but to tell her. 'He's been there before.'

Her head was shaking and so was her whole body. 'No,' she said, 'he can't be.' Her eyes were glistening and I knew that tears weren't far away.

I held her firmly by the shoulders and spoke directly at her. 'Listen,' I said, 'I need you to calm down. The boys are upstairs so I need you to look after our sons while I go over and see if he's still there.'

'What if he is?' she asked.

If I'm honest I hadn't given much thought to what came next, so I shrugged my shoulders. 'I'm not sure,' I admitted. 'I guess I'll go over and see what he wants.'

'*Talk* to him?' she made it sound like a ridiculous idea.

'Don't worry,' I assured her. 'It'll be fine.'

'What does he want?' the wobble was still in her voice and the tears that had been in her eyes were now rolling down her cheeks.

'I don't know,' I said as I pulled her close again. I could

see the reflection of her face in the hall mirror as she rested her head on my shoulder. She looked terrified. I squeezed her and said, 'but whatever it is, I'm going to find out.' I kissed the top of her head and patted her back. 'Don't worry,' I said, 'I'll not be long.'

I didn't like leaving her, not in the state she was in, but I had to go. Anyway, Michelle is the strongest person I know so I was confident that she'd pull herself together once I had left, if only for the boys' sake. She'd be mortified if one of them came downstairs and saw her like that.

She stood in the doorway and watched me get into the car. I noticed that she was hanging on to the jamb and I thought it was probably to stop herself from falling down. I waved at her before I drove off but she didn't wave back. She probably didn't dare let go.

I pulled the hand brake on and turned the ignition off outside the house. We're talking about summer but it was late into the evening and the light was fading. Even so, I could still make out the shape of a Fiesta parked up the street. Streetlights caused shadows and all I could make out was the shape of a person sitting in the car. I could see the silhouette of their head and shoulders and that was all I needed. I would have known that shape anywhere.

I sat, I watched, and I waited.

Eventually I climbed out of the car and, as I did, I caught a glimpse of my dad at one of the bedroom windows. After locking the car door, I put the keys in my pocket and started to walk slowly towards my brother.

I was about six feet away before I could see him clearly. As he came into focus, I could see that time had apparently been good to him and he seemed to have changed very little. A bit heavier maybe but, other than that, he looked pretty much the same as he had the last time I had seen him.

ROBERT

'Do it,' Angie said to me the following week, I think it was a Wednesday. 'Go, knock at the door and say "here I am".'

I started to say something but didn't get the chance because she put her finger on my lips.

'No Rob,' she said sternly, 'this is eating you up and it has to stop.' She put her hands on either side of my head and with her face about an inch away from mine said, 'Promise me you really will do it this time. Promise me that you'll at least say hello to your mother.'

I promised her I would and all the way there I believed I could do it. As I drove I asked myself what was the worst that could happen? Would she close the door in my face? I doubted it, though I couldn't be sure that she would welcome me with open arms. It had been so long and I had left so suddenly. If Michelle had given the baby up for adoption maybe she would resent me for robbing her of a grandchild. What if no more had come along and, because of me and my selfishness, she had not had the chance to know her only grandchild?

I hadn't given her or anyone else another thought when I'd left. I'd done it because it was what was right for me. I know that I had been selfish leaving that way – I've never denied that – and the closer I got to home, the more I doubted that she would forgive me for it.

If I was being honest, I still wasn't sure why I was

doing this: why was even thinking about going back home? Why had it suddenly become important to me? There had to be more to it than me wanting my mother's forgiveness. Wouldn't that be the most selfish thing that I had ever done? Was I really prepared to risk hurting her all over again by dragging up a load of 'what might have been' just because I'd decided it was what I needed? Maybe it would be better to cut and run before anyone realised I'd even been there.

I almost pulled off a junction early, just so that I could go around the roundabout and join the motorway going in the opposite direction. My hand was actually on the indicator when Angie's face popped up in front of my eyes. I'd promised her that I would at least say hello to my mum and I didn't think I could face her if I hadn't.

I arrived mid-afternoon but instead of going straight to the house and getting it over with I parked the car near the Town Hall and went for a walk. The town had changed during my absence and as I walked up the High Street I wondered if I would ever see anything that I recognised. The sports shop was now a charity shop and the cinema was a pub. I went inside and ordered myself a pint of bitter. I also ordered a burger and chips, which I was thankful took a long time coming; anything to put off what I had promised to do.

It was standard pub chain fare but what do you expect for less than a fiver? I was tempted by another pint but the last thing I needed to do was turn up blotto so I had a coffee instead.

It was just before six when I stepped back onto the street and walked slowly back to the car. I was still tempted to just get back on the A1 and go home but at the back of my mind was this little niggle of the promise I had made to Angie.

I took my phone out of my pocket and rang her just so that I could hear her voice. We spoke for a couple of minutes about nothing in particular and before we said goodbye I told her not to wait up. Then I spent almost two hours driving around and it was just five to eight when I pulled into what I was starting to regard as my spot outside number six.

Just do it, I told myself, *just knock on the door,* but something stopped me. I cursed myself for being a coward but I still sat where I was, looking at the house. It was only after everything happened that I realised how lucky I'd been that one of the neighbours didn't ring the police and say that there was someone casing the street – maybe they need to start a Neighbourhood Watch scheme.

A light came on in the living room at about half eight and, not long after, in one of the front bedrooms. A couple of minutes later, someone – I couldn't tell who – closed the curtains. It looked like Mum was settling down for the night and I thought that I might have left it too late. Maybe I would book into a hotel for the night – I was sure I could find one somewhere – and come back the following day to keep my promise to Angie.

I'd just decided that was what I would do, when I saw it was too late. Tom's car was moving up the street and into position outside our childhood home. *Sod it,* I thought but, in a way, I was pleased. My hand was being forced and maybe that was what I needed. He got out of his car and started to walk slowly towards me.

He looked good. His hair was shorter and, dressed in jeans and a leather jacket, he looked even younger than he had the other day. It popped into my head that I'd bet he still got asked his age in pubs – if I didn't know him I'd certainly have questioned his age. He'd always hated looking younger than he was. His face was the same but there was something different about him. He walked with purpose now, like a man in control of his life.

He stopped about six feet away and looked at me. I thought I could see the muscles in his face twitching. He stood with his hands in his pockets waiting for me to make my move.

TOM

I stared at him, defying him to make his move. I noticed that his eyes flicked momentarily in the direction of our parents' house and I wondered if someone had opened the door or maybe even come into the garden. I didn't check: I didn't want to give him the chance to drive away.

His eyes came back to mine.

Eventually he opened the door and unfolded himself out of the car. He never broke eye contact.

'Tom,' he said from where he stood behind the open door.

'What do you want?' I asked.

He gave a little fake laugh and said, 'Whatever happened to "it's good to see you"?' He had a smile on his face… well, I'm calling it a smile, but there was nothing real about it. It was so obviously forced.

'It's not,' I said. I heard that my voice had risen and I fought to keep it under control. 'What's wrong? Is this not the welcome that you were hoping for?'

Annoyingly, his voice was calm as he said, 'It's good to see you, Tom. You look well.'

I hated the fact that he was able to control himself. I tried to do the same but when I asked, 'What do you want, Robert?' I didn't think that I quite managed it.

Robert looked over my shoulder and I *knew* that something was happening behind me. I didn't turn around to see what. I heard footsteps approaching and I felt my dad by my side.

For the first time Robert's smile seemed genuine when he looked at our father and said, 'Hello, Dad. How have you been?'

'What do you care?' Dad sounded angrier than I had ever heard him before.

'I care,' Robert said slowly. He looked at me too and repeated, 'I care.'

I've heard people talk of times when they could cut the tension with a knife but I'd never thought that it could happen. As I stood there with my dad and my brother, it felt possible.

'Come on,' Dad said as he turned. He added, 'Both of you,' as he started to walk away.

I started to say something but he was quick to cut me off.

'This isn't the place, Tom.' He looked at us in turn, 'Let's get this over with.'

Robert locked his car and started to follow Dad. I drew up the rear so that I could keep my eye on him. When we got to the gate, Robert stood with his hand on the wrought iron that had seen better days. I pushed past him and went to the door where my mother was waiting.

I noticed a glint in her eyes as she looked beyond me to where Robert was. As I came up beside her she forced herself to smile at me and she mouthed something that I couldn't make out. She put her hand on my arm and I patted it. Then I went into the house, leaving her to welcome back the child that she probably thought she had lost for ever.

The son in me really despised the fact that my mother was clearly going to welcome Robert back so willingly but, like I've said before, the parent in me realised that it was always going to be that way. That didn't mean I wanted to witness it though, so I left them to it.

I joined Dad in the living room where he was sitting in a chair to one side of the fireplace. I sat on the chair opposite, leaving the sofa free for Mum and her Number One Son.

Dad and I looked at each other and after a few seconds he tried to smile at me.

'It'll be OK, son,' he said, though I could barely hear the words because his voice was so low.

I could only nod my head because I didn't trust myself to say anything. My stomach was flipping over and over and I felt sick. This was the day that I had feared would come and now that it had, well I just wished to God it hadn't.

We heard the door close and Mum and Robert murmuring to each other. I couldn't hear what they were saying but I could hear the tension in Robert's voice which gave me hope that maybe some of his previous cockiness had been knocked out of him over the years. Perhaps the calmness I'd witnessed in the street had been a façade.

He stood in the doorway but didn't immediately come into the room. Mum appeared at his shoulder and urged him on. 'It's all right,' she said. I thought she was underestimating the situation.

Robert had his eyes down as he walked the three or four steps to the sofa and sat down. Mum perched herself on the edge of the seat beside him.

No one spoke for what felt like hours.

Mum's hand seemed to hover over her knee. Occasionally it would twitch towards Robert like she was desperate to touch him but was afraid that if she did she might find out that he wasn't really there. Her right foot bounced which caused her to rock slightly. She held her bottom lip between her teeth and her eyes were fixed on her son.

Robert flicked his eyes towards her once or twice but looked uncomfortable under her scrutiny. He looked at Dad a couple of times but he didn't look at me.

I was sitting forward in the chair, resting my elbows on my knees. My hands were joined together loosely and I moved my thumbs around each other. I wished someone would speak.

I decided that if my world was about to fall down around my ears I would rather face it head on than wait for it to tap me on the shoulder, so I decided to get on with whatever was coming. I lifted one hand to my face and covered my mouth, pinching my nose hard. I held my breath and my nose for a few seconds before letting them go.

'So,' I asked, 'where did you go?'

My question seemed to take him by surprise. The way that he turned his head and looked at me, it was as if he had forgotten that I was there.

'The coast,' he said vaguely before quickly looking away.

'Where?' I don't know why that was the question that I wanted answered but it was. I know you'd think that the more pertinent question would be 'why' but it wasn't. '*Where* on the coast?'

Robert gave a vague shrug of his shoulders, rolling his head to the side at the same time.

'Does it matter?' Mum asked, looking at me properly for the first time. It was the only time in several minutes that she had taken her eyes off Robert and that in itself felt like a small victory.

Now that I had her eyes I grabbed them and held them. 'Not really,' I said, 'I'm just curious.'

Robert gave a nervous cough and, turning his attention to Dad, repeated what he had said outside. 'How have you been?'

This time, Dad said, 'I'm not so bad.' But his answer was just as vague as Robert's had been and I wondered if he was playing him at his own game.

'You were though, Dad, weren't you?' I thought I'd elaborate on his answer. 'You were ill.'

'But that's all over now,' Mum said quickly. 'He's fine now. The doctor says that with a bit of rest he'll be fine.'

I wanted to say that an ongoing lung condition wasn't 'fine' but out of the corner of my eye I caught Dad looking at me and his eyes were telling me to keep that thought to myself.

'And you, Mum?' Robert seemed to have relaxed a bit.

'How have you been?'

'Oh, I've been fine,' she said softly. 'You know me, I never ail a thing.'

'That's good.' I was watching his face and I saw Robert's lip twitching. He turned his head slowly in my direction and asked. 'What about you? How have you been, Tommo?'

The use of the childhood nickname annoyed the hell out of me. When he'd addressed the note he'd left me in that way I'd seen it as an act of brotherly love, but to hear him speak it then felt like an insult.

'Good,' I said, as an involuntary smile broke over my lips. 'I've been good, thank you very much.'

I watched his Adam's apple bob up and down as he swallowed hard. It was obvious that his mouth was dry and he ran his tongue over his lips. He took a couple of deep breaths. I was looking at him intently, making it clear that I was waiting for his next question.

'What did you do after college?' he asked.

He seemed genuinely surprised when I said, 'I didn't finish college.'

'Oh,' he looked a little embarrassed when the noise just popped out.

'I decided it wasn't for me,' I said, enjoying how uncomfortable the conversation was making him.

'He went to Lodge's,' Mum said in a bright and breezy tone that I think was meant to diffuse the tension that was brewing.

Robert pursed his lips, nodded his head and feigned

interest. 'Good company,' he said. 'You still there?'

'No,' I said, though I didn't offer him any more than that.

Mum looked at me and I could see the irritation written all over her face. She inched towards Robert. 'What about you, Robert?' she said. 'What have you been doing? Do you still work in a garage?'

'No,' he said and his mood seemed to change. 'Believe it or not I'm a pub landlord.'

'Oh,' Mum gushed, not even trying to hide the pride from her voice.

'It's not a big place,' Robert told her, 'but it's doing all right. I started out working behind the bar, then I was made manager, and when the chance came I bought it.'

Robert visibly relaxed as he told Mum about his pub but once that subject had been exhausted the tension returned. I have to tell you that I enjoyed seeing him at a loss and I was in no mood to make him feel more comfortable. He allowed his eyes to brush over the room. Maybe he was trying to see if it had changed. It hadn't really, apart from a change of colour on the walls, oh and the artwork of course. His eyes rested on the photograph that had pride of place over the mantelpiece.

'They yours?' he jutted his chin in its direction.

I thought it was a bloody stupid question – who else would they belong to. In the interests of being civil I just said, 'Yes.'

'Nice looking boys,' he said and, to be fair, the compliment sounded genuine. Then he said, 'They must take after their mother,' but only Mum laughed at his attempted joke. 'No seriously, Tom,' he said, engaging me directly for the first time, 'they are good looking boys. How old are they?' My stomach tightened as I knew that the truth would shortly be out.

'Simon's sixteen, Anthony's thirteen and Michael's eleven,' I told him and left it at that.

'Simon's waiting for his GCSE results,' Mum announced and I was irritated that she had singled him out.

'And Michael starts St Charles' in September,' Dad said and I was aware that his comment was more a show of support to me than an offer of information.

Robert hadn't taken his eyes off the picture. It was like he was weighing something up. 'What about Anthony?' he asked. 'What makes him special?'

'There's nothing special about any of them,' I said. 'They're just my sons.'

'You must be proud,' Robert's tone softened and there was even a hint of a smile on his face as he looked at me: the first real one he'd sent in my direction.

'I am,' I hoped I didn't sound as defensive as I felt.

'And your wife?'

It took all my strength to keep my voice calm, 'She's proud too.'

'I'm sure she is,' he laughed, 'I meant who is she? Do I know her?'

'She's called Michelle,' I said, and out of the corner of my eye I saw Mum's hand cover her mouth.

ROBERT

There was something about the way that Tom was looking at me. Something that I hadn't seen before. Something I can only describe as grown up. He had been little more than a boy when I left but there was a man standing in front of me that night. He'd taken a step to the side so that he was literally standing in front of the car like we were playing chicken or something. I felt like he was daring me to run him over. Obviously, I wasn't going to do that so I got out of the car.

The flippant part of me wants to tell you that it was like a scene from a cowboy film. Two gunslingers standing in the street facing each other, waiting to see who would draw first.

Sorry, I shouldn't make light of it because it was clear that he was angry with me and he had every right to be. He'd probably got earache off everyone for months after I left.

We had a brief conversation that was basically a series of monosyllabic grunts that got us nowhere and then I saw him: Dad. He came out of the gate and started to walk towards us. I can't tell you how relieved I was that Dad hadn't died while I was away. I honestly don't think I could have lived with myself if what I had feared had been true.

Anyway, Dad being Dad, he told us both to get in the house and I immediately felt like a child again. He just said it, turned away and expected us to follow. Tom started to say something but he was soon put in his place.

Mum was waiting in the doorstep and, honest to God, I thought I was going to burst into tears when I saw her. As I saw her rest her hand on Tom's arm I realised for the first time what an impossible position I had put her in. Tom hadn't hidden the fact that he didn't want me there and I had a feeling Dad would be on his side. But what about Mum? I realised that I was forcing her to make a choice and I don't think I've ever hated myself more than I did right then.

Dad and Tom had disappeared into the house and I stood on the doorstep with my mother. She lifted her hands to my face and rested them on my cheeks.

'Oh, Robert,' she said before throwing her arms around my neck and pulling me in close. I buried my face into her neck and hugged her. I took a deep breath to get the smell of her into my lungs.

Neither of us wanted to be the first to let go, but when we eventually did release each other she took my hand and tried to pull me towards the living room. I tried to tell her that I wasn't sure it was a good idea.

'You've done the hard bit, son,' she whispered. 'Don't worry about Tom and your dad. They'll come around.'

I wished I shared her optimism but she was right; I had done the hard bit and if I wasn't going to see it through, what had been the point in me coming?

Dad and Tom were sitting either side of the fireplace. I flopped down onto the sofa and Mum sat next to me. Out of the corner of my eye I could see that she was dying to touch me and I prayed she wouldn't. I didn't see any way that it would help the situation.

I'd tried asking my dad how he was when we were outside and he'd said something like, 'Why do you care,' but I did care; I'd feared he was dead for God's sake, so of course I cared. I asked him again and this time he said he was all right, but Tom pitched in and said that he had been ill. Mum tried to dismiss it as nothing but I saw Tom's face and I wasn't so sure. It crossed my mind that maybe I had come back just in time. Some invisible tie between us had pulled me back. It sounds daft now, but I wasn't really thinking straight.

I got a shock when Tom said he hadn't finished Art College. I'd imagined him scraping a living doing something arty like making jewellery, so when Mum told me he'd taken a job at Lodge's I was genuinely surprised. If I'm honest I've never known exactly what they do, but they had flash offices in the centre of town and I knew they paid well. He told me he wasn't there anymore but wherever he was now he must have fallen on his feet because he looked well, he dressed well and, when I got a closer look at his car, I saw it was less than two years old, which made it a damn sight younger than mine.

When Mum asked me what I did, I tried to play it down a bit but she was still impressed. She went all 'Ooh, a pub landlord' on us.

I made a point of looking around. Anything to stop Mum banging on about the pub. The last thing I wanted to do was make it look like I was boasting. The room was almost exactly the way that it had looked the last time I was there. The walls were a slightly different shade of magnolia and I was almost certain it was the same three-piece but with new covers. However, above the mantelpiece was something that told me just how far my little brother really had come.

Three boys smiled down on us from a three-foot by two-foot canvas, and each of them looked like Tom. I'd noticed that he wore a wedding ring but I hadn't mentioned it until then. I said he and his wife must be proud of them and he said they were. I'd already asked him how old his sons were and his answer set alarm bells ringing. When I asked him about his wife and when he told me her name was Michelle I realised that maybe the eldest boy might not look like my brother after all.

TOM

The house was in darkness when I pulled the car onto the driveway. I glanced at the clock on the dashboard and was surprised to see that it was after midnight. I'd no idea that it had got so late. I turned the engine off and sat in the darkness, replaying the last few hours over and over in my head.

After a couple of minutes my reverie was broken when I caught sight of movement to my left. It was Michelle. She was standing in the doorway with the light from the hall casting a glow around her. She wrapped the dressing gown that she was wearing tightly around her waist and pulled viciously on the belt. I quickly got out of the car and went to her. I put my arms around her and felt that she was shaking. I tightened my grip on her shoulders but it was some minutes before the shaking stopped. Eventually I loosened my grip and managed to manoeuvre her back into the house. I let go of her just long enough to close the door and lock it behind us.

I stared at the amber liquid in the glass that I cradled loosely in my fingers. Michelle had poured more than she would normally and I was able to follow the sip that I had just taken all the way down to my stomach by the slight burn it left behind. I knew that Michelle was looking at me but I continued to stare at my whisky.

I lifted the glass up to my mouth and took another drink. I held the liquid in my mouth until my tongue tingled. I didn't look up, but I did speak.

'He said we had good looking boys,' I told her.

'What?' Michelle's voice was shaky and a bit screechy like she couldn't believe what I'd just told her.

I put the glass down and, finally, lifted my head to look at her. I repeated what I had said.

Michelle was holding a glass of vodka and tonic in her hand and as she tried to put it on the coffee table her hand shook so much that the glass rattled against the wood. When it was eventually down she slipped off her seat and almost crawled across the floor towards me. She put her hands on my knees and squeezed them. 'How does he know what they look like?' she asked.

I dropped onto the floor to sit with her. 'The photo on the wall,' I said. As I stroked her hair I saw the question in her eyes. I knew what she was thinking.

She grabbed hold of my wrists. 'Did...?' she was struggling to breathe and that was all she could manage.

'No,' I said, 'he didn't ask.'

I saw relief flow over her face but that was swiftly replaced by something else. I think it was disbelief.

'He didn't ask about...?' I knew what she meant even if she couldn't bring herself to say it.

'No,' I assured her as I brought her hands to my lips and kissed them.

She looked puzzled and I think her mouth was starting to form the word 'how?'.

I saved her the bother and said, 'He's still the same selfish bastard that he always was.' I could understand her disbelief because, in his shoes, I was certain that I would have worked out that there was something different about Simon and I don't think I could have stopped myself asking *the* question; I would need to know. Not that the shoe would ever have been on the other foot because I would never have done what he did.

Michelle allowed herself to flop against the chair she was closest to. She rested her elbow on the seat and planted her head on the palm of her hand. She started to pluck at her fringe and then she ran the hand she wasn't leaning on over her head, taking her hair with it. The shake of her head was almost invisible.

'No,' she said.

'No, what?'

She pushed herself upright. 'No, it can't be that easy.'

She clearly knew my brother better than I had ever given her credit for because I was almost certain that it couldn't be that easy either. Robert had come back now for a reason and I wouldn't settle until I knew what it was. This wasn't over by a long shot.

We went to bed but, late in the night, when neither of us had slept, we finally faced each other in the darkness.

'What are we going to do?' Michelle asked.

I lifted myself up onto my elbow and looked down at her. Even in the dark I could make out her face and see that she was terrified. 'We're going to face him,' I said.

She squeaked a noise that might have been a word but it

was hard to tell. I held her.

Next morning, we got up as usual and tried to make the day as normal as we could.

Simon was meeting a mate in town, making the most of the last days of freedom before getting the dreaded GCSE results which would shape his future. He'd asked me the morning before if he could cadge a lift and I'd said yes but he had to be ready to leave just after eight. He was downstairs by five to.

'I'll see you tonight,' I told Michelle as I put my jacket on. She nodded her head slowly and forced a smile onto her face. I kissed her gently as she stood on the doorstep waiting to see us off. Simon was already waiting at the car with a look of mock disgust on his face.

'Shouldn't you two pack that in?' he said. 'Anybody could see.'

I laughed at him and told him to get in the car.

For a while we drove in silence until Simon asked, 'Is Grandad all right?'

'Why wouldn't he be?' I asked.

'Isn't that why you went round last night?' I felt him looking at me but I kept my eyes on the road.

'He's fine,' I said, paying more attention than was required to the traffic lights we'd stopped at.

'She was crying last night you know.'

I turned my head sharply but now it was his turn to look at the lights. 'Was she?'

'I wouldn't have said it otherwise, would I?'

I expected him to add 'duh' to the end of the sentence but he didn't. For once I let the stroppiness go. The car behind me honked and, when I checked, the lights had already turned to green. I waved an apology before moving on.

'She went to have a bath,' he went on, still looking out of the window. 'Maybe she thought I couldn't hear her over the music but I could. I could hear her sobbing so I thought that it had something to do with you going to Gran's house.'

I didn't tell him what had actually upset his mother; I just reassured him that his grandfather was all right, as was his gran for that matter.

'So why was she sobbing?' he asked. 'You two had a row?'

'No,' I made it sound like it was a ridiculous idea. 'I know she's your mum, but she's a woman first and foremost and if you want my advice you won't bother trying to understand them. Crying makes them feel better, don't ask me why, it just does.'

'Maybe it was something at work,' Simon said. 'She must see some horrible stuff at that hospital.'

I made a noise that sounded as though I was agreeing with him and left it at that.

Simon put his headphones in and we travelled the rest of the journey in silence. I felt something in my chest, something that felt like a brick. Simon was a bright lad and I knew that we wouldn't be able to fob him off. Would it be so bad if he knew the truth? It would be better than carrying a brick around in my chest for the rest of my life, and I would rather the truth came from us than someone else.

I pulled the car into a space near the library so that Simon could get out. He climbed out but before he closed the door he leaned in and smiled at me.

'Thanks, Dad,' he said. 'See you later.'

I was his dad, he was my son, and I had to trust that that would be enough.

Michelle looked horrified when I suggested we should tell him that evening. 'It's the only way,' I told her. 'Think about it, at the minute we are both terrified of the truth. Robert's not stupid, he'll have worked out that you are the Michelle that I'm married to and that Simon is…'

'Simon is not his son,' she hissed.

'No, he isn't,' I took hold of her hands, mainly to stop her from pulling her nails off. 'Simon is my son, but Robert was his sperm donor.' I used the term that she had used years earlier, even though I hated the sound of it. 'But Robert will work out the truth and the last thing we want is him telling Simon. We are his parents and we should be the ones to tell him.'

Reluctantly she agreed. The phone rang about five minutes after. It was Mum.

'What's wrong?' I asked.

'Robert wants to talk to you,' she said.

'Does he now?' I said sarcastically. 'Well, if Robert wants it…' I didn't finish the sentence.

'Don't be like that, Tom,' she said. 'It's not easy for him either.'

I didn't trust myself to say anything so I waited for her to speak again. I didn't have to wait long.

'He wants to know if you'll meet him on Saturday.'

I didn't see that I had a choice, not really, so I agreed. Saturday was two days away and we decided to hold fire on speaking to Simon until after we had spoken to Robert.

When I got to the pub where I had agreed to meet Robert, he was already standing at the bar watching the door. He smiled at me when I walked in. The smile soon disappeared when Michelle walked in after me.

ROBERT

Mum saw me to the door

'Don't worry,' she whispered as she opened it for me, 'they'll come around.' She nodded her head towards the room where we had left Dad and Tom.

I wished that I could share her confidence. Tom was a chip off Dad's shoulder and they were as stubborn as each other.

'Oh, son,' she said stroking the side of my face. 'It's good to see you.'

'You too, Mum.' I put my hand on her face too. We hugged.

'Where are you staying?' she asked. 'You could stay here if you want.'

I had to laugh at that one. 'I don't think so, Mum,' I said. 'I'm going to drive home, I'll be there in a couple of hours.'

We hugged again before I left and I could tell that she was reluctant to let me go. I told her that I'd be back soon. I took a step away from the door, just one, and then I turned around.

'Mum,' I said cautiously, not really knowing if I wanted her to answer my question. 'Michelle…?' I didn't really know what it was that I wanted to know, but Mum did and she answered my question without saying a word. I just had to look at her eyes.

I needed Angie. I called her after I left my parents' house and said that I was on my way home. She said that she'd be waiting up for me. I played music loud on the drive home, anything to stop me thinking about what had happened.

True to her word Angie was still up when I got home. She was sitting on the sofa with a bottle of wine open on the table in front of her. I took my jacket off and threw it on the back of a chair as she filled a glass and slid it along the coffee table until it was in front of the seat next to her. She poured herself a glass too and waited for me to join her. She didn't say anything, she just sat and sipped until I could put my thoughts into words.

Do you know what I said first? It's funny really.

'Dad's not dead.'

That made her smile and she said that she was pleased to hear it.

However, I followed it up with, 'but I think I'm dead to him.' And that wasn't quite so funny.

Angie watched and waited for me to explain.

'He could barely look at me.'

'Give him time, Rob. He'll come around,' she said but that was easy for her to say. She hadn't seen the look on his face or heard the pain in his voice.

'Maybe,' I conceded but I wasn't sure. I'm going to say that I laughed when I told her that Tom and I had had a stand-off in the street but it wasn't a real laugh, it was more a nervous reaction. 'I thought he'd be pleased to see me…' I said pathetically, 'but he wasn't… he said as much.' I strung my words out with pauses between them. 'Dad dragged us into the house... Mum was waiting for me. At least she seemed happy that I was there.' I took a large slug of the wine that Angie had poured me. It was a bottle of what we called 'the good stuff', a two-year-old cabernet sauvignon. 'Tom's changed,' I said and emptied my drink. I reached for the bottle and refilled my glass.

'In what way?' Angie drained her glass too and held it out for a top-up.

'He's settled down,' I said. 'I'd half expected him to be spending his time drinking lager shandies and scraping a living painting pictures of dogs, but instead I found that he wears a suit and drives a sensible car. He's not the free spirit I thought he'd be; he's a family man.'

Angie raised an eyebrow and I nodded, confirming that she had heard me right.

'He's married with children. They were in a picture hanging in pride of place over the mantle-piece. Three boys, all teeth and blond hair smiling for the camera.' I knew my words had a sour note to them. I hadn't meant it to come out that way. I know that Angie detected it too but she ignored it.

'So, three nephews. How old are they?'

'I'm not sure,' I admitted. 'I think he said that the younger ones were eleven and fourteen.'

'Younger ones?' She'd been about to take a drink but she held the glass a good few inches short of her mouth and asked, 'So how old is the eldest?'

I lowered my eyes and said, 'He's sixteen.' I couldn't

look at her. When I think back on it now, I realise it was because I feared that even though she didn't know everything yet, she would somehow work out what I thought I had.

I found myself yet again staring at a drink. She didn't say anything for a few seconds and neither did I. A growing feeling of something momentous hung between us.

'Sixteen...?' she said eventually, stretching the word out so that it sounded like a question.

'Yes,' I said, forcing my head up to look into her eyes. 'And guess what?' I waited a second or two to see if she was going to have a pop at guessing. She didn't. 'Tom's wife is called Michelle.'

'Wow! Is...?' She didn't know quite how to put the question but I knew what it was.

'I don't know,' I said. 'I could hardly ask "is that the same Michelle that I used to go out with?" could I? "Is that the same Michelle that I got pregnant?"' I immediately wished I hadn't said it because Angie visibly flinched.

She began to digest what I'd told her. 'So, do you think it *is* the same Michelle?' she asked, but I knew that what she really wanted to know was, *is that eldest lad yours?*

I took a deep breath. 'You know me Angie,' I said, 'I'm not big on coincidences and all I know is that Tom wasn't seeing anyone called Michelle when I left and I'm willing to bet my life that he wasn't sleeping with anyone back then either. And now he has a sixteen-year-old son. What do you think?'

'He might have been seeing someone that you didn't know about and, come on, it's not like Michelle is a rare name.'

I shook my head. I knew what she was saying was possible, in theory, but I knew she wasn't right. The look in Mum's eyes when I'd almost asked the question had been all the confirmation that I'd needed. 'She didn't come after me for money,' I said, 'because my brother married her. Why would he do that? I never asked him to marry her. I asked him to look out for her if he got the chance, that's all... "look out for her", I said.'

Angie stared at me – right at me – like she was trying to look into my mind or something.

I hated myself as soon as I'd done it but I snapped, 'What?' at her. 'What do you want me to say?'

'I don't want you to say anything,' she said. She didn't try too hard to hide the anger from her voice and I didn't blame her.

'Sorry, Angie,' I said. 'I shouldn't take it out on you.'

'No, you shouldn't,' she said firmly. 'I'm not the one you're angry with.' She knew me so well and I admitted to her that she was right. She let me think on that for a second or two and then she asked. 'Who are you angry with?'

'I don't know,' I said, rubbing the palms of my hands over my face.

She was determined to get a better answer out of me. 'Are you angry at Michelle because she got married?' she asked, letting it rest a second or two before saying, 'or are you angry at Tom because he married her?'

'We don't actually know yet that she married my brother.'

When she looked at me I thought I saw pity in her eyes and I didn't like that. The last thing I wanted was her pity – or anyone's, come to that.

'No, we don't,' she said, 'which is why you need to find out for sure.'

I knew she was right.

The next day I rang Mum.

'Oh, it's lovely to hear from you,' she said and I could just tell that she was smiling as she spoke.

'Mum,' I said, unsure of how to broach the subject, 'will you ring Tom for me?'

'Tom?' she sounded surprised. 'Why?'

'Because he's my brother,' I said, 'and I need to build bridges.' I suggested that she ask him to meet me in a pub on Saturday afternoon. Judging by the suit and the car I thought he was a Monday to Friday sort of bloke so would be free on a Saturday afternoon. She said that she would call me back after she had spoken to him.

Tom agreed to meet me. We had arranged to meet at three but I was there just after half two. I parked under a tree and looked around at the other cars. I couldn't see Tom's. I gave it five or ten minutes and then went in, ordered a pint and waited.

TOM

We were holding hands when we walked in and I felt Michelle's grip tighten as soon as she saw Robert standing at the bar. I squeezed her hand back, trying to reassure her.

The girl behind the bar asked what she could get us. I ordered a pint and a large white wine.

'I'll get those.' Robert had his hand in his pocket and whipped a fiver out which he handed over the bar. Part of me wanted to say no but, at the end of the day, a white wine was the least he owed Michelle.

There was a free table a couple of feet away and I put my hand on the base of Michelle's back and directed her towards it. She turned when I touched her and I saw how tense she looked, especially around her mouth. I could have sworn I saw her bottom lip quivering. I winked at her to try and put her at ease and hoped that she realised how much I loved her. I wanted her to know that I was there to support her. My wife is a strong woman but I knew that seeing my brother again would be a major test for her. I rubbed my hand up and down her spine and when I mouthed the words 'I love you' she seemed to relax a bit.

As she mouthed 'I love you, too' the muscles around her mouth relaxed enough to form a smile.

I pulled a chair out and Michelle sat down. I took the chair beside her and I tapped her knee as I sat down. Robert turned from the bar and carried the drinks over. I noticed that he held the three glasses easily between his hands. He set them on the table and sat in one of the two chairs opposite us.

'Thanks for coming,' he said, and immediately took a sip of beer. I didn't answer him. If he'd looked at me he would have seen me nod but his eyes were down as he drank. If I hadn't known him better, I'd have said he looked embarrassed.

A period of silence followed and, I'm not going to deny it, it was awkward. Eventually I had to ask the question that had kept me awake for the previous two nights. 'What do you want, Robert?' I asked.

'Who says I want anything?' he asked, though he failed to carry off the characteristic cockiness I think he was trying to achieve. He turned his attention to Michelle and I thought I saw the look in his eyes soften. 'You look good, Chelle,' he said and immediately realised he shouldn't have called her that and apologised.

'I *am* good,' she said as she made a point of turning her head and smiling at me.

We spent the next ten minutes dancing around the details. He asked me about my job and I asked him about his, though I couldn't have cared less about what it was like to own a pub. He said he was pleased that Michelle had returned to nursing. It was all just meaningless small talk to fill the silence.

'How long have you been married?' Robert glanced at each of us in turn like he wasn't asking either of us in particular.

I answered for us. 'Nearly seventeen years.'

He did that thing where you nod your head and screw up your lips which told me that I had just confirmed something he had assumed. I didn't want him to dwell on it so I asked, 'What about you?' Are you married?'

'No,' he said. There was a smile – or was it a smirk? – on his face when he told us, 'Angie and me never got around to it.'

'How long have you been together?' Michelle asked. I doubt she was really interested; I got the feeling that it was just something to say.

'A long time,' he laughed, 'fifteen years or so.' He took a sip of his beer before he said, 'You'd like her,' directly to Michelle. I think he realised that I didn't care about his love life.

Another awkward silence was followed by what we knew would come.

'So,' Robert said, trying to sound casual, 'you have three boys.'

'Yes, we do,' Michelle said defiantly.

Silence. I couldn't stand it. 'Look Robert,' I said, 'just ask what you want to know.'

He smiled, genuinely smiled, at me. 'You haven't changed, Tom,' he said. 'Straight to the point as usual.'

I shrugged my shoulders. It was true; I'm not a fan of pussy-footing around.

'All right,' he said. He took a couple of deep breaths before he asked, 'Is Simon mine?'

Before I could get a word out Michelle beat me to it.

'No, he's not.'

I looked at Robert's face and I saw that, just like Michelle's had been, the muscles around his mouth were tense, so much so that I could actually see him twitching. He turned his attention to me and I suspect that my facial muscles were betraying me, too. I certainly felt strained enough.

'You're lying,' he said. He sat upright and pushed back on the chair. 'You're lying,' he repeated as he shook his head and switched his eyes between us and his near empty pint of beer.

'Why would I lie, Robert?' Michelle asked. There was something worryingly calm about the tone of her voice. 'You left me with nothing but a note and some bad memories.'

His eyes stopped flicking to the beer and rested on my wife. 'What about the baby you were expecting?'

'What baby?' she spat. 'The one you wanted nothing to do with?'

He started to say, 'Come on, Chelle,' but she cut him off before he was even half way though the words.

'Don't "come on, Chelle" me,' she hissed through gritted teeth. I had never seen her so angry before, and she was more than a match for my brother. She had over sixteen years of pent up anger to get rid of.

Although he spoke the truth, Robert really shouldn't have gone on to say, 'You were pregnant when I left.'

'Yeah, well, you weren't bothered about that then so why are you bothered about it now?'

Michelle lifted her glass to her mouth and emptied about half of it down her throat. God love her, she's not much of a drinker at the best of times, so I feared for what she might say once the alcohol took effect. Not that I made any attempt to stop her. Why should I? She was entitled to this moment. I think wanting to have that conversation was why she had insisted on coming with me that afternoon.

'All I want to know is,' Robert said slowly, 'am I Simon's father?'

'And I have told you,' Michelle said just as slowly and emphasised every word, 'no, you are not.' She put her trembling hand in mine. I squeezed the tips of her fingers and hoped that it told her that I was one hundred per cent behind her. 'You *were* the sperm donor if that's what you want to know,' she tapped the table with the index finger of her spare hand, 'but you are not Simon's father.'

'Semantics,' he said as he glared at her. He turned away and said, 'I'm getting another drink. Does anyone else want one?'

I shook my head and said I was driving.

'Very responsible of you, Tom,' he said as he stood up and I couldn't help feeling he was sneering at me. I felt my legs starting to push me up but Michelle must have felt it too because she exerted extra pressure on my hand.

'Don't bite,' she whispered.

Michelle said she would have another white wine but just a small one this time and, while Robert waited his turn at the bar, we put our heads together and whispered.

'Are you all right?' I asked.

221

'I'm sorry,' she said, and for a split second I was scared because I didn't know what she was apologising for. If I'm being truthful, it did cross my mind that she was going to tell me something that I didn't want to hear. My fears were allayed when she said, 'I didn't mean to lose my temper.'

I laughed at her. 'Don't be daft,' I said. 'You're entitled to be angry.'

'I know, but I didn't want to let him get under my skin.' She managed to get the words out just before Robert put a glass down in front of her.

'Cheers,' he held his glass up and saluted us. 'So,' he said after a large gulp of his new pint, 'fair play to you, Tom.' There was more than a hint of mockery in his voice, 'It's not every bloke who would take on another man's baby.' He let that hang a second or two before adding, 'especially when that other man is your brother.'

I felt Michelle's nails sticking into my hand which was enough to curtail my desire to smack him in the face.

'I don't know what I ever saw in you,' Michelle told him. 'You make me sick.'

That seemed to take the wind out of his sails because Robert always thought he was God's gift and my guess was that no one had ever said anything like that to him before. But it bothered me that he seemed to care what she thought about him.

'Does he know?' Robert asked, once he'd recovered himself.

Michelle and I looked at one other, an involuntary action that told him everything he needed to know. By the time we looked back at him, he was shaking his head.

'He doesn't, does he?' He gave a little laugh and looked at each of us in turn. 'I think I'd like to meet him,' he said and, even though I'd half expected the suggestion to be made, I wasn't ready for it. I felt sick.. 'I'd like to meet all of your sons,' he said, though that did nothing to make the feeling go away. I knew that it was Simon he wanted to see.

I suppose we could have said no, told him he couldn't, but the genie was out of the bottle and I doubted that the boys' mythical Uncle Robert would disappear again just because we wanted him to.

'OK,' I said reluctantly, 'they've heard about you and I'm sure they'd like to put a face to the name.'

He sounded surprised, 'You told them about me?'

'Mum talks about you,' I told him.

We agreed that he could meet our sons but we didn't set a time or a date. We left shortly after and drove home in silence. My eyes were on the road ahead but every now and then I would flick my eyes to the left and, each time I did, I saw that Michelle was staring straight ahead. Her hands were on her lap but they were restless, moving over each other, pulling at each other and I thought that they probably reflecting what was going on in her head.

I almost spoke, before realising that I had no idea what to say. I didn't want to ask her any questions that I didn't want to know the answers to.

Simon was staying at his mate's house that night and

Michelle's parents had suggested that they keep the other two at their house overnight. Her mum had said something about giving us some space after the meeting with Robert and I for one was pleased that we wouldn't have to face the kids right away. Having said that, the house was unnaturally quiet when we went in, which was a bit unsettling.

We were barely through the door when Michelle announced that she was going for a bath and disappeared up the stairs without a backward glance. I watched her until she was out of sight before I went into the living room and flopped onto the sofa. As I lay there I wondered what Michelle was thinking about as she lay in the bath.

She hadn't seen Robert in almost seventeen years and, if I'm honest, I'd been worried that something might have rekindled. She hadn't said or done anything to make me think that, but the niggle was still there. Even after all these years, there were still times when I asked myself what I had done to deserve her. God, I hated my insecurities.

I thought about Robert. They'd been close once – *very* close. There had been an attraction between them so it would be understandable if it was still there. Feelings had lain dormant for years but now that they'd seen each other again maybe those feelings... I couldn't even bring myself to finish the thought.

It occurred to me that right at that moment perhaps Michelle might be trying to work out how she was going to tell me that she'd realised she still loved Robert. My heart was beating like the clappers and I could feel beads of sweat forming on my forehead. She'd told him that she despised him, she'd said that he wasn't Simon's father. She'd said that, but... what did it matter what she'd said? It was what she was thinking and what she was *feeling* that worried me.

I covered my eyes with my arm and let all manner of things go through my head: every fear, every thought, every doubt that I'd had in the last seventeen years. I didn't know what I would do if my nightmare came true.

It was well over an hour before I heard the bath draining. Michelle came downstairs a few minutes later wrapped in a towelling dressing gown with her hair combed tight to her head.

She gave my feet a tap and I lifted them up so she could sit down next to me. She looked like she'd been crying. She pulled my feet onto her knees and started plucking at my socks.

'We need to talk,' she said, without taking her eyes off my feet.

My stomach flipped as I waited for her to start – it felt like a long time before she eventually spoke. She chose her words carefully.

'What does this mean for us?' she asked. She turned her head to me and I could see that there were tears sitting in the edge of her eyes. I lifted my feet off her knee and sat up. I moved close to her and as our legs touched I felt her knees knocking against mine. She was clearly just as petrified as I was. I put a hand on her knee and held it still.

'What does it mean for us?' she said again, though the

second time it was barely more than a whisper.

'It doesn't mean *anything* to me,' I spoke with more confidence than I felt, 'not as far as we're concerned anyway. It means nothing to us as a couple, if that's what you mean.'

'But he's back,' she said.

'More's the pity,' I lifted her hand to my lips and kissed her palm. 'But we always knew it could happen.'

She wiped her eyes with the heel of her spare hand, leaving a red mark across her cheek.

Now that it appeared she wasn't going to tell me her old feelings for Robert had returned, my confidence grew by the second. 'His coming back doesn't change anything between us,' I said. 'You are still my wife, the mother of my children, and I love you very much.'

She looked deep into my eyes and said, 'I love you too, Tom. More than I think you realise.'

That was all I needed to know. Robert coming back would obviously make a difference to our lives but it would not change us. I know I was naïve, but as long as I had Michelle I knew that I could face anything that the world – and that included Robert – threw at me.

ROBERT

I hadn't expected Michelle to be there, so of course I was surprised when she walked in. I'd assumed it would just be me and Tom. At least it saved me the bother of asking him if his wife was the girl I had left behind all those years ago. There she was, looking almost the same as she had the last time I'd seen her: marriage and motherhood clearly suited her.

I couldn't help noticing that they were holding hands and as soon as I saw that I felt a knot form in my stomach. I'd expected that she would have moved on, I just hadn't expected her to move on with my brother.

He ordered drinks but I said I'd buy them. It seemed like the right thing to do seeing as I was the one who had made the invitation. Michelle had wine, which surprised me because she'd been strictly a lager and lime girl when I knew her. I guess she had changed.

The conversation was stilted to say the least and I put my foot right in it when I called her Chelle. I hadn't meant to, it just popped out. I did it without thinking because it's what I'd always called her. I apologised but it was too late and, if such a thing were possible, I'd made a bad situation even worse.

I asked how long they'd been married and when Tom said almost seventeen years it was all the confirmation I needed. However, the truth just presented me with another problem and I wasn't sure how to proceed. I made a comment about them having three boys and Tom got straight to the point and asked me what I wanted to know. I'd spent much of the week imagining the moment that I asked 'the question', wondering how I would react when I found out the truth. But Tom had given me the opportunity, so I took it and asked straight out if Simon was my son. I hadn't anticipated the answer I got. Michelle looked me in the eye and told me I wasn't.

I called her a liar. Well, I didn't use that word – I said she was lying, which amounts to the same thing. She asked me why she would lie. I asked her what had happened to the baby that she was having when I left, I got nowhere with that, so I asked her outright again if I was Simon's father. She said no again and, to be fair, when she explained it, I got what she meant. A father provides for their child – you know, feeds them, clothes them, things like that. She admitted that I was his 'sperm donor', but there was no way I was his father. I hated that, hated the way it sounded. Like it or not, I knew she was right. I hadn't shown any interest in the baby; I'd buggered off to avoid having anything to do with it, so what right did I have to ask if he was mine?

I needed another drink, and I asked if anyone else wanted one. When Tom said that he didn't because he was driving I made a snide comment about him being responsible. Terrible, I know. And then, as if that wasn't bad enough, I said something about him taking on another man's baby. But I didn't even stop there, and I added

228

something about that other man being his brother. I wasn't proud of myself for that but once the words were out it was too late, it had been said.

Michelle said that she didn't know what she had ever seen in me and I almost laughed at that. She just wanted to hurt me, and she knew exactly how to do it.

I said that I wanted to meet Simon but quickly realised that I had to extend the invitation to the other two lads as well. I'd never had nephews before and I genuinely wanted to meet them, but I wanted to meet my son more. Even the sound of the word 'son' in my head felt weird. Wanting to see him felt very real, I wanted to see how he'd turned out. I thought that they'd put up a fight but they didn't.

I was surprised when they said that the lads knew about me. It pleased me, but Tom soon put me right and said that Mum talked about me. Good old Mum. I knew I could rely on her.

We didn't make definite plans or any plans at all but Tom's a man of his word so I knew that the meeting would take place.

They left the pub before me but were only just leaving the car park by the time I left five minutes later. I saw the back of their car disappearing through the gate and around the corner as I walked across the tarmac.

I didn't set off straight away either, I sat in the car staring straight ahead and trying to come to terms with why I felt the way that I did. I'd left... No, let's be honest... I'd run away, because I didn't want anything to do with the baby Michelle was having. And when Angie had persuaded me that there was no baby I was happy, so why was I so interested in him now?

I thought about that all the way home.

We left the pub in Colin's capable hands and sat together in our flat as I told Angie everything that I could remember about the afternoon. She'd asked me to tell her 'word for word' what had happened and I did the best I could.

After I'd finished talking I could almost see the cogs going around in Angie's head as she worked out what she thought.

'How did you feel when you saw her?' she asked.

'Surprised,' I said, 'I thought I was just meeting Tom.' I could tell from the look on her face that she hadn't meant it that way. She wanted to know *how* I had felt. I shrugged my shoulders and admitted, 'I don't know. She looked just about the same as she did before. Her hair's a bit longer but apart from that she's barely changed.' Still not what she was looking for so I stopped beating about the bush, 'If you mean did I look at her and think *Oh my God I wish I'd never left her behind* or *I still love her* then the answer is no. I'm not going to lie to you Angie, it felt a bit odd seeing her holding hands with Tom but it would have been odd seeing him hold hands with anyone. He's my little brother for God's sake.' She looked sceptical but I assured her that I was telling the truth, and I was.

She's a good listener and Angie watched and waited until I was ready to talk some more. She's been in the pub trade long enough to know when someone needs to talk.

You have to be a good listener and she was one of the best.

The thing about someone waiting for you to talk, you know, just sitting there waiting is that eventually you talk. 'If you'd been a fly on the wall,' I said, 'you'd think I sounded bitter. I know I sounded bitter. Thinking about it now, I know that's how I sounded but that's really not how I'd meant to come across. I made a comment when I went to buy a drink that I wish I hadn't.' I could feel Angie's eyes on me all of time but I mainly kept mine on the floor. Now that I'd started talking I wanted to tell her everything and I couldn't get the words out quickly enough.

'I made a snarky comment about him being very responsible because he didn't want to drink and drive.' I think I might have smiled at that point because, on the inside, I was laughing at myself and my own stupidity. 'I didn't leave it at that though,' I told her. 'No, I had to make this clever comment about it being just like him to take on another man's child. And then, I went further. I said, "especially when that other man is your brother".'

I felt pretty ashamed once the story of how I'd behaved was out there, and I didn't dare to look at Angie in case I saw disappointment in her eyes. I was disappointed enough in myself; to my dying day I'll never know why I said what I did to Tom that day. He didn't deserve it.

I went to the cupboard that we kept the whisky in, poured myself a double measure and added the tiniest drop of water. I poured Angie a Bailey's and carried the drinks back to where she was still sitting.

As I handed her the glass she asked, 'Why did you say

231

it?'

'Honestly?' I asked as I sat down. 'I was trying to be funny.' The whisky felt good in my mouth. 'You know me, Angie,' I said, 'I'm a confident bloke, always have been. I know who I am and I know what I want, but this afternoon my confidence deserted me.' I took another sip of whisky as I told her, 'I was trying to make a joke but it just came out sounding spiteful.'

'Did you apologise?' she asked.

'I don't think so,' I admitted. 'I think that was when Michelle said that she didn't know what she'd ever seen in me and I don't blame her.'

'You were a different person then,' Angie said, though it did little to make me feel better.

'What the hell's wrong with me?' I waved my hands about as I asked the question. 'My brother is happy, I should be pleased for him.'

'You've just found out that you have a son,' Angie pointed out but I knew that was no excuse.

'A son I didn't want anything to do with.' Even I could hear the flatness in my voice. 'I'd hate me too.'

That was the eureka moment. I realised I was jealous.

TOM

'He says he wants to meet Simon,' I said quietly. Dad and I were sitting together in the living room but I had an idea that Mum might be listening just outside the door, waiting for the right time to make her entrance. She'd said she was making tea but she was taking her time about it.

She chose that exact moment to come through the door carrying a tray so I'm pretty sure that my guess was right.

'What are you two whispering about?' she said as she put a mug in front of each of us. She placed the tray on the floor, picked up her own mug and asked, 'So how'd it go then?'

I looked at Dad and then I looked at her. She was sipping her drink but she couldn't hide the smile on her lips. Why was she smiling? I didn't understand it. What was she hoping I would say? That we had mended fences and buried hatchets? I could tell her where I'd like to bury the hatchet but I didn't think she'd like it. If she'd been hoping for reconciliation over a pint of bitter she was going to be sorely disappointed.

I couldn't help looking at the photo above the fireplace as I repeated, 'He wants to meet Simon.'

'Oh?' she said, lowering her mug and resting it on her knees. 'And how do you feel about that?'

'How do you think?' I snapped. .

There was an awkward silence.

'Well,' Mum said, sipping at her tea again, 'it's only to be expected I suppose.'

'Why is it?' She opened her mouth but I didn't give her time to say anything. 'He gave up any chance of being Simon's dad when he pissed off and left Michelle high and dry.' I didn't apologise for the bad language.

'All I meant, Tom,' her tone was more gentle after my outburst, 'is that you can understand it.'

I opened my mouth to speak but this time it was her turn to silence me. She held her hand up in that way that says *shut up*. 'Of course you're Simon's dad, but all I'm saying is that you can understand Robert wanting to meet him. You'd want to if it was you who…'

'I would never have left in the first place,' I said, cutting her off in mid-sentence. 'He had his chance to be a father to Simon but he didn't want that. He hasn't given a stuff about his child for sixteen years but now that he's decided that he wants to meet him, we're supposed to go along with what he wants.' I paused just long enough to breathe. 'And we have to go along with it, don't we?' I heard my voice getting louder with each word. 'Because if we don't, he might turn up on our doorstep one day and introduce himself.'

'He wouldn't do that,' Mum said. She took a sip of tea and looked at me over the rim of her mug. She lowered the mug without breaking the eye contact. It was like she was defying me to disagree with her.

Her plan worked and I backed down, on the outside at least. Inside I was still as mad as hell. 'To be fair to him,' I said, though God knows why I should be fair to him, 'he said he wanted to meet all of the boys... but I'm not sure he meant it.'

'Of course he meant it, they're his nephews,' she said cheerily. I wondered if she actually believed what she was saying.

'Like it or not son,' Dad, as usual, was the voice of reason, 'he's back now. He knows about you and Michelle and he knows about Simon. You have done nothing to be ashamed of. You and Michelle are happy and you have made a lovely family together. If you want my opinion I'd say get the thing over and done with.'

'That's why I'm here,' I said. I took a sip of my tea and turned to my mother as I set the mug down. I deliberately ignored the coaster and put it straight on the table. I saw her eyes flick towards it and her lips pursed tightly. 'Ring him,' it wasn't a request, 'he can meet them here next Saturday.'

'Wouldn't Sunday be better?' she suggested. 'I mean, he might busy in the pub on a Saturday. He's already missed one Saturday at work.' I didn't trust myself to say anything so I just looked at her. 'I'll ring him,' she conceded.

As I drove home, Mum's words echoed in my head, 'Of course you're Simon's father,' she had said. She'd even sounded like she meant it.

The smell of pork roasting in the oven welcomed me home, followed quickly by Michelle.

'Well?' she kissed me briefly and stepped away so that she could look at my face. She always said that my eyes give me away when I'm lying.

I gave a non-committal shrug. 'I told Mum to ring him and say that he can meet the boys at their house next Saturday.'

'Who?'

We turned at the sound of Anthony's voice. We hadn't realised that he was on his way downstairs.

'Who are we going to meet?'

'Just your uncle Robert,' I tried to make light of it.

'Really?' He sounded excited by the prospect. Then he laughed and said, 'I didn't think he really existed,' before disappearing towards the kitchen and asking, 'How long till dinner?'

I'd felt Michelle tense up when Anthony appeared but she recovered enough to say, 'Half an hour.'

Anthony shared his news with his brothers when they assembled around the dinner table.

Michael was more interested in the plate that his mum had just put in front of him, but Simon asked, 'Why?'

'Because he wants to meet you.' I didn't elaborate.

'No, what I meant was,' Simon held the gravy boat in one hand as he asked, 'why now? Where's he been and why's he back all of a sudden?'

'Oh, I don't know,' I said lightly, 'he decided that he wanted to come back so he did. Maybe he was missing us.' I tried to make it sound like it was nothing special.

'Couldn't have missed us that much,' Simon said as he

drenched his food with gravy, 'or he wouldn't have stayed away so long.'

The talking stopped when we all had full plates in front of us and I was glad of that.

Later, when the meal was over and the boys had disappeared, Michelle and I stood in the kitchen doing the dishes. She washed them carefully and I dried them slowly.

'Are we still going to tell him?' Michelle asked as she handed me a plate.

I nodded my head and said, 'We have no choice. He should hear it from us.'

'Maybe Robert wouldn't tell him.' I think she said it more in hope than expectation.

I put the plate I'd been drying down, put my hand on her shoulder and said. 'We can't take the chance.'

She nodded her head slowly but didn't say anything. She knew Robert almost as well as I did. He would do anything if he thought it was to his advantage.

The GCSE results were due out that Thursday so we decided to wait until after that before we said anything.

Thursday brought nine A stars, an A, and a B. The results were beyond what any of us had expected and I think I can include Simon in that. He seemed as amazed as we were. And proud. We let him have Thursday, but the following day Michelle's mum and dad took the younger two to the pictures and we prepared for the conversation.

Simon sat between us on the sofa and looked at each of us suspiciously. 'Are you two getting divorced?' he asked.

I could see that Michelle was as surprised as I was by that question and we both laughed and said, 'No,' at the same time.

'So, what's this about then?' he asked. 'Why am I sitting here while they're at the cinema with gran and grand-dad? Obviously there's something going on.'

Michelle had already said that she didn't think she could say it, so I took a deep breath and dove in. 'You're right,' I said, 'there is something that we wanted to say to you.'

I realised that I should maybe have started the conversation with something different, something that didn't sound quite so serious. I should just have said that we wanted a chat but I hadn't, so I had to deal with it.

'What...?' he lengthened the word and he looked really worried.

Now that the time had arrived I wasn't sure that I could do it. No, that's not right, I knew that I *could* do it because I had to, I just didn't know *how* to do it. I didn't know the right words to use. 'It's about your uncle Robert,' I said, giving myself a little time to think.

'What about him?' he still sounded suspicious. 'Is this where you're going to tell me he's been in the nick for the last seventeen years?'

I laughed at that and wondered where that idea had come from. 'No,' I said, though part of me wished that it was. It would have been easier.

'What then?' He looked at each of us in turn, 'Oh, come on,' he said, 'just tell me. It can't be *that* bad.'

Sometimes there is nothing to do but just spit it out and,

for me, this was one of those times. I watched for his reaction as I said, 'He's not your uncle.'

He looked more intently at us and then it was as if a lightbulb had gone on in his head and he turned to his mother and asked, 'What's *he* talking about?' I couldn't help thinking that he emphasised the word 'he' a bit too much.

Michelle looked over his head at me. She was pale and there were tears forming in her eyes. I could see her swallowing hard. I tried to send confidence through the air to her and it must have reached her because she gave a little nod of her head and then spoke slowly. 'I used to go out with Robert and we'd been together for a little over a year when I discovered that I was pregnant… with you.' When she paused I could see that her lips were trembling. 'The day after I'd told him, I came home from work to a letter… a letter from Robert. He said that we would both be better off without him.' She couldn't hold the tears back any longer and one escaped and rolled down her cheek.

Simon turned to me. 'What does she mean?' he asked.

'She means exactly what she said,' I told him. 'Robert left a note for your mum, another for me, and one for your gran and grand-dad. He didn't tell anyone where he was going. Your grandparents and I didn't even know why he had gone at first; he just left. We didn't see him or hear from him until a few weeks ago.'

Something had occurred to Simon and his eyes screwed up as he thought it through. 'Is that why you went to gran's house late that night?' he asked. He didn't get all those A stars without being a bright lad.

'Yes,' I said.

My heart went out to him as he stared at the floor. 'I don't understand,' he said slowly. 'I thought you were my dad.'

I put my hand on his shoulder. 'I *am* your dad, Si.' My head was close to his and I spoke directly into his ear. 'Always have been, always will be.'

'So... why...?' He didn't appear to have the words to say what was on his mind so I helped him out.

'The thing is that my brother is, well, a bit of a knob if I'm honest and he always does what's best for him. Once he discovered that me and your mum were together he worked out that you were the baby that your mum had been expecting when he left. I'm not just saying this, but if he thought it would benefit him somehow he'd put an advert in the paper announcing that he was your dad. We didn't want you to find out that way.' My hand was still on his shoulder and I pulled him close to me as I said, 'We wanted to be the ones to tell you.'

Normally I would have met at least a little resistance when I hugged him, but not that day. He just leaned his head against my chest and asked, 'Why didn't he want me?' His voice had become childlike.

'He didn't know you,' Michelle said. She had regained some of her composure and she put her hand on Simon's knee. I couldn't see it but I think her other arm was around his back. It was like we had formed a barrier around him. 'You weren't a person to him,' she said, 'you were something that he didn't want to be involved with at that moment.'

'And what about now?' Fear had replaced the child in his voice. 'Does he want to be involved with me now?'

'We don't know,' Michelle said, 'but he has asked to meet you.'

'Just me?' More fear.

'All of you,' I told him. 'He said that he wants to meet all of you.'

'When did he say that?'

Michelle and I looked at each other. There was no point hiding anything from him, not now, we'd gone too far for that.

'When we met him last weekend.'

Simon's mouth formed a W but I didn't give him chance to ask why, where, or whatever else he was thinking of.

'When you and Matt were staying over with Philip, we asked gran and grand-dad if Michael and Anthony could stay with them so that we could meet him in the afternoon.'

He was quiet for a few seconds. His breathing was heavy like he was struggling within himself. Hardly surprising, I suppose. It's not every day that you get news like we had just given him. Obviously Simon had to be the one to lead the conversation, so we waited until he was ready to speak.

'How did you feel when you saw him?' he asked Michelle eventually.

The question took her by surprise and she gave some

thought to her answer. 'Weird,' was what she came up with. She stared at the top of Simon's head as she tried to explain. 'I trusted him way back then, but he showed me that he couldn't be trusted. So when I saw him again I saw someone who had let me down and, more importantly, let *you* down. It was like meeting up with someone I used to know, but someone that I would happily never have seen again.'

'Did you love him?' I thought that the question was a bit intrusive but Michelle took it in her stride.

'Yes,' she said, 'once upon a time I loved him very much.'

'Do you still love him?'

'No.' Her answer came without hesitation, 'I haven't loved him for a very long time.'

'And what about Dad? Do you love him?'

I couldn't help noticing that he had called me dad. Habit?

'Yes,' she stroked his hair but she looked at me. 'I love him very much.'

Simon's head twisted under his mother's hand. 'Do you love Mum?'

'More than I can tell you,' I said. I let that sink in a second and added, 'And I love you too.'

'Even th—?'

I cut him off before he could ask the question. 'Even though anything,' I said.

The look in his eyes suggested he wasn't sure if he believed me or not.

242

'Look,' I told him. 'I knew your mum while we were at school. When Robert left the way that he did, I went to gran and grand-dad's house to check how she was and we started to spend time together. We found that we enjoyed each other's company and the more time we spent together, the more I liked her. It didn't matter to me that she was pregnant. I once told her that you were a baby and not a spare head.' I looked at Michelle as I paused to draw breath and she encouraged me with a look and a smile. 'I loved her as a person,' I said, looking at Simon again, 'and I asked her to marry me because I loved her. You made us complete.'

'But I...'

I think I know what he was going to say, but he didn't get the chance. 'You were my son,' I said, 'from the minute you were born.'

He stood up slowly and left the room without looking at either of us.

The sound of his feet running up the stairs seemed to echo through the house, as did the sound of his bedroom door slamming.

Michelle and I looked at each other and I saw that she was distraught. I put my arms around her and let her cry against my chest.

'He hates us,' she said softly.

'No he doesn't,' I told her, though I thought that he might. 'He's just confused and maybe a bit angry.'

'Yes,' she said, lifting her head up so that she could look at me, 'angry... with us.'

I pulled her back into me. 'He'll come around.' I tried to sound like I believed what I was saying.

'I'll go and see him.' She tried to pull away from me but I held her tight.

'No,' I said, 'leave him.' I was relieved that she didn't object so I suspected that she hadn't really wanted to go to him, she'd just thought it was something she should do. 'Give him a bit of time and then I'll go and see him.' She started to object but I said, 'I was a sixteen-year-old boy once. I know how they think.'

I knew I was stretching it a bit by that statement, because while I may have been a sixteen-year-old boy once, I'd never been told that my dad wasn't my dad so I didn't really know what Simon was thinking. I just didn't want him taking his anger out on his mum.

When she had recovered a little and stopped crying she pushed herself away from me and grabbed a handful of tissues. She stuffed the wad into each eye socket in turn and then blew her nose. Even with puffy eyes and a red nose she was still beautiful.

'Did we do the right thing?' she asked as she threw the tissues in the vague direction of the waste bin.

'Yes,' and I said it with conviction. 'We did the only thing that we could.'

'Maybe Robert really had no intention of telling him.' I think even she knew that she was clutching at straws.

'Maybe he didn't,' I agreed and as I said it Michelle looked horrified because she realised that we might have turned Simon's world upside down for no reason. 'But you know as well as I do that if Robert had thought there was something in it for him, he would have told Simon himself. Maybe not tomorrow, but it could have been the day after, or the next week, the next year. Would you really have wanted to feel like you were being held to ransom for the rest of your life?'

Her mouth made the shape of *No* but no sound came out.

We gave Simon an hour before I went up to him. I tapped gently on his bedroom door and said, 'Simon? It's me. Can I come in?'

There was no answer.

I knocked again, harder this time. I only had time to say his name before I heard him snap, 'What?'

Any other time I wouldn't have suffered that from him, but he deserved a bit of lee-way that day so I let it go. 'Can I come in please?' I asked.

He didn't answer straight away but eventually he said, 'Do what you like.'

I opened the door cautiously and popped my head round. He was lying on the bed facing the wall with his back to me.

Simon has a small desk that he uses for doing his homework and I pulled the chair from under it and put it next to the bed near his head.

'Are you all right?' I asked.

He didn't say anything and after a few seconds I went to put my hand on his shoulder but I'd barely touched him when he shrugged it away. I sat on the chair with my elbows on my knees and my hands joined between them. I settled down and prepared to wait.

There is a clock on Simon's wall and I watched ten minutes pass before he shuffled around, first onto his back and then onto his other side so that he was facing me. I could see that he had been crying. His eyes were dry but he couldn't hide the redness. He pushed himself up onto his elbow.

'Why?' his voice croaked. There were so many things he could have been asking about that I had no idea how to answer it until he was more specific. 'Why didn't he want me?'

I took a deep breath and chose my words carefully. 'It wasn't you he didn't want. Like your mum said, you weren't a person to him.'

My heart went out to him because you only had to look in his eyes to see how he was struggling with what we had told him. There were the raised red veins that spoke of the crying he'd done, but more than that, his eyes were wide and a bit manic. And they were flicking around like he was searching for something. I knew he wouldn't find his answers in the shadows so I waited for him to ask his questions, intending to answer them as honestly as I could.

'How could he leave Mum like that?' In that question he told me everything I needed to know about the way he felt about his mother. If no one else, he still loved her.

It was a question that I'd asked myself a thousand times before but I'd never come up with an acceptable answer. I shook my head slowly and said, 'I don't know.'

He pushed himself into a sitting position and lifted his knees towards his body. He wrapped his arms around his legs and rested his chin on top of them. He was taking long deep breaths. After a minute or so of silence he turned his head so that he faced me with his cheek resting where his chin had been. 'Did you marry Mum because of me?' He sniffed hard.

'No,' I said, 'I married your mum because I loved her.'

'But it must have bothered you, even if just a little bit.' He sounded like he'd just lost about ten years in age.

I tried to explain it to him by saying, 'What bothered me was that Robert had left your mum. I couldn't understand how anyone could walk away from her. Like I said, I'd known her at school but only as someone who was in the same year as me, someone that all the lads in my year admired from afar. After we left school I didn't see her for a few years, then one Friday night we happened to find ourselves in the same pub. Unfortunately, my brother was there too and while your mum and I were chatting and I was plucking up the courage to ask her if I could buy her a drink, he got in there like a rat up a drainpipe and asked her out before I could. I was so angry with him. Then, after he left her in the lurch, I wanted to make sure she was all right. I didn't go with the intention of stepping into his shoes, I just needed to know she was OK, but the more time I spent with her – the more I got to know her – the more I realised she was everything I'd ever wanted. I couldn't imagine life without her. The fact that she was bringing you along with her was a bonus.'

He smiled for the first time since I'd gone into the room.

'So why has he come back?' he asked, 'What does he want?

I shuffled right to the edge of my seat so that I was as close to him as possible. 'I don't know why he's back or what he wants, but if it's you, he's going to be disappointed. *You*,' I emphasised the word, 'are *my* son as far as I'm concerned. I was there when you were born, and the first time that I held you I thought that my heart was going to burst with how much love I felt. You weren't officially mine then, but in every other way you were. You were less than a year old when I adopted you, and that was a day we all celebrated. I have never loved you any differently to your brothers, I have never thought of you as any less a part of me than either of them, and to the day I die I will always think of you as my son.'

He closed his eyes and asked, 'I don't have to be his son too, do I?'

My eyes had a prickly feeling and I couldn't trust myself to say anything. We looked at each other for no more than a second before I moved onto the bed and hugged him. I don't know how long we sat like that but I could have stayed there for ever.

At some point we heard the sound of Michael and Anthony coming through the front door talking excitedly, but we still didn't move. I was willing to be there for as long as Simon needed me.

'We'd better go and hear about this film,' he said eventually, patting me on the back as he spoke.

'Can't wait.' I nodded my head and tried to make a joke of it. I put the chair back where I'd found it and Simon pushed himself off the bed and checked himself out in the mirror. It was one thing dropping your guard in front of your dad, but you couldn't let your little brothers see that side of you. I watched him looking at himself. He seemed happy with what he saw but when he ran his fingers through his short hair my stomach turned. I had seen Robert do it just like that hundreds of times before.

He saw that I was looking at him and he used the mirror to look at me. 'What's he like?' he asked.

I gave that a bit of consideration as I leaned against the door with my hand on the handle. 'He used to be my hero,' I said. 'When we were little I wanted to be him.' It sounded like a ridiculous notion now that I was saying out loud. 'I felt like such a jerk beside him.' I could feel a smile on my face as I thought about that other lifetime. 'People always said that we looked alike and I suppose we did. He was a bit taller than me, but we weren't really alike in any other way. He was the outgoing one, I was the one in the background. He was the one going out with his girlfriend and I was the one still hanging around with my mates.'

I hadn't realised that he wasn't looking at me through the mirror anymore. He had turned around.

'Am I like him?' he asked.

'No,' I said, 'not really. He was a cocky little sod.'

I started to twist the handle but he stopped me in my

tracks by asking, 'Do I have to be nice to him?'

'Not on my account,' I said.

We left the room and at the bottom of the stairs I went towards the kitchen, where I could see Michelle sitting at the kitchen table looking anxious, and Simon went into the living room where his brothers were. 'All right,' I heard him say, 'which one of you is going to tell me all about it.'

I heard both of them start telling him at once and that's when I realised that Simon wasn't like Robert at all. Robert had never given a shit about what I thought about anything.

ROBERT

I was pulling a pint when I saw Angie come through the door that led from our flat. I was surprised to see her because it was officially her day off and she avoided the bar like the plague when she wasn't working. I'd handed the drink over, taken the money and dropped it in the till by the time she got to me.

'Your mum's on the phone,' she said. She took the drink order from the next customer in line and I climbed the stairs two at a time. Mum had never called during opening hours before so I thought something must be wrong. Dad being ill again came to mind straight away and my heart was in my mouth. The phone was resting on the coffee table and I sat down, just in case, as I put it to my ear.

'Mum?'

She didn't say hello just, 'She sounds nice.'

'Angie?' daft question because who else could she mean. 'Yeah, she's good. You'd like her,' I said.

There was a bit of a pause and then she hit me with it. 'So, you met Thomas yesterday,' she said.

It struck me as an odd thing for her to say so I reminded her, 'You knew I was meeting him. You set it up.'

The silence told me that she was huffed by my comment. I was sorry about that and I said so.

'I hear that Michelle was there too,' she said. I think

she'd accepted my apology so I wondered if she sounded peeved because of Michelle.

'Yeah,' I said, 'I hadn't expected to see her so it was a bit of a surprise.'

I think she was expecting me to expand on that but when I didn't she had to force the issue.

'And how was it?'

In my mind my mother was standing with her arms crossed over her chest.

'It was fine,' I said. 'Difficult in places but, given the situation, it was fine. It was never going to be easy. Too much has happened.'

She made a comment about it not being fair that Michelle had come with Tom. 'It should just have been the two of you,' she said. 'That was what was arranged.'

'But she's his wife, Mum,' I said, and as I heard myself saying the words they sounded right. I realised that I was reconciled to their marriage. Michelle was nothing to me now other than a sister-in-law. To be honest, they did make a nice couple and, on reflection, she was much more suited to Tom than to me.

'So, you know about Simon,' she said after another brief silence.

'Yes.'

'Tom says that you want to meet him,' she almost sounded like she didn't believe what she had heard.

'I said I wanted to meet all the boys,' I clarified, though I'm sure Mum knew that I was hiding behind the younger boys. I mean, yes, I was interested in meeting my nephews but my son was my main concern.

'Why?' she asked. That also struck me as odd because I thought she of all people would have understood.

'He doesn't know about me,' I said, though I couldn't pinpoint why that mattered.

There was a longer pause and when Mum finally spoke her tone was quiet and serious. 'Tom has done a good job bringing him up, you know,' she said. 'He has never treated Simon any differently to the other two and there's many a man that would have. There's many a man who would have singled the lad out and thrown him back in his mother's face every time they had a row.'

I'm ashamed to say that the thought *All hail St Tom* ran through my mind at that point before I realised that Mum was still talking.

'Simon loves Tom and he is the only father that the lad has ever known. Anyway,' with the lecture over she gave a heavy sigh and said, 'Tom was here earlier and he's asked me to tell you that you can meet them here next Saturday.'

I'm not going to deny that being told where and when I could meet Simon irked me a bit but, at the end of the day, Tom was holding all the cards. I told her I'd be there. 'Bring that lass,' Mum said. 'I'd like to meet her.'

The bar was busy when I went back down so it wasn't until much later that I was able to tell Angie what Mum and I had spoken about.

'She said you should come too,' I told her. 'She thinks that you sound nice.'

Angie didn't seem keen at first, citing the fact that both

of us being away on a Saturday afternoon during the high season might be too much.

'Please,' I said, 'I want you there. Colin and Danny will be fine, especially if we get his niece in to give them a hand. She did all right before and I'm sure she'll jump at the chance of a few hours.'

'I'd feel like I was intruding,' she said. 'Shouldn't it just be family?'

The words, 'You *are* my family,' were out before I realised it. They surprised me a little bit but they surprised Angie more. 'You should feel honoured,' I laughed, 'Mum's never asked to meet one of my girlfriends before.' She started to protest again so I told her, 'I want you there,' and that was enough.

'OK,' she said with a smile.

The upcoming meeting was on my mind pretty much all of that week. I wondered how I would react when I saw Simon for the first time. How could I not treat him differently from his half-brothers? He *was* different. He was my son.

Angie knew me well enough to know what would be going through my head and she wasn't afraid to give me her opinion.

'I know finding out that you had a son must have come as a shock to you,' she said the night before we were due to meet, 'but your brother is his father. Tom has been his father for over sixteen years and Simon will love him... as a father. Do you really want to destroy everything that he

254

has ever known?'

That had given me some food for thought and I was still thinking on it as we set off the following lunchtime. I knew that she was right but it all came down to the fact that we all deserve to know where we came from, don't we?

As the miles passed, her words kept coming back to haunt me. *Your brother is his father*, she'd said. Well it was true that he had brought Simon up but it was my DNA that was in him. He was my son. Biologically *I* was his father.

Father.

The word sat there in my mind and made me think about my own dad. I remembered how I'd felt when I'd thought that Dad might have died while I'd been away. I don't think I could have forgiven myself if my fears had been true. I had been so relieved to see him coming out of the house that night and walking towards where Tom and I were eyeballing each other.

We hadn't always seen eye to eye and I was fully aware that I had ruined our relationship by my actions seventeen years earlier, but we had been close when I was growing up.

He had been there, standing on the edge of the pitch on wet Saturday mornings, shouting me on even though I was never quite good enough to make the first eleven. When I fell out of a tree when I was eight years old he was the one who had taken me to the hospital and stayed with me while they reset the bone. He even bought me a remote-controlled car for being brave. When I had needed him, he had been there for me. When Simon needed his father, it was Tom he had turned to.

Maybe the best thing that I could do for my son was to let my brother go on being his dad.

SIMON

It's been ten years since that first meeting with the man that I had called Uncle Rob.

He'd come into Gran's with his girlfriend and even now I can remember the anticipation in the air. Was it anticipation? For my brothers maybe, but probably not for my parents. For myself, I'd been worried that there would be a connection between us, you know, some sort of bond between two people cut from the same cloth. I didn't want to feel anything but... Anyway, I think Mum and Dad had been worried about it too because I could feel their eyes on me, looking for my reaction as soon as Rob appeared in the doorway.

I was relieved when there wasn't one. I looked at him and all I could think was *so you're the bloke who did the dirty on me and my mum.*

He was the one who introduced himself. *Hello, boys. I'm your Uncle Rob*, he said and the phrase *Rob the knob* popped into my head. Michael and Anthony both piped up a greeting but I didn't. I looked at him and defied him to say something to me. Eventually he said *You must be Simon.* I said I was and he said he was pleased to meet me. He said he was pleased to meet us all but I wasn't sure that I trusted him enough to believe him.

Why should I trust him?

He put an arm around the woman he was with and

introduced us to Angie. I took a sly look at Mum out of the corner of my eye, trying to gauge if there was a reaction. To me it looked like she couldn't care less who her ex-boyfriend had his arm around.

Gran told them to sit down while she put the kettle on and made a pot of tea. It's her answer to any tricky situation. She asked me to give her a hand carrying things in.

'You all right love?' she asked when we were alone.

'Yeah, I'm fine,' I said. I don't know what else she expected me to say. Did she think I was going to ask her if what my parents had told me was true? Yeah well, I didn't ask her anything. I didn't give a toss who Uncle Rob really was.

She had two trays already prepared and all that was left to do was actually make the tea. She flicked the switch on the kettle and it immediately made a sound that told me it had been very recently boiled. As soon as the kettle turned itself off she warmed the pot, then poured the water into the teapot and put the lid on. She put the pot on a tray with a matching milk jug and sugar bowl that I had never seen before. She asked me to take one tray and said that she would bring the other.

I hadn't really noticed what was on the tray that she was going to carry but when I saw that it had matching cups and saucers on it I couldn't help being annoyed. We'd only ever got mugs before and yet as soon as *he'd* turned up the good stuff came out. What the hell was that all about? Didn't we deserve the good stuff too?

'Shall I be mother?' she asked when both trays were on the coffee table. 'Do you still have one sugar in yours, Robert?'

'No,' he said 'Just milk, thanks.'

Gran's hand shook so much that the cup rattled on the saucer as she handed it to him and he at least had the good grace to look a bit embarrassed that he was being served first.

On that occasion tea did little to make the situation better. They all sat on the edge of their seats sipping out of the best china.

Gran kept calling him Robert but he told her that everyone called him Rob these days. 'Really?' she said, like it was something random that he would make up. Angie laughed and said that she'd never heard anyone call him Robert before. Gran's face looked like she was sucking on a lemon when she heard that. She said that it would take a bit of getting used to but she would try and remember. I can tell you right now that I have *never* heard her call him anything but Robert.

Rob made a point of asking Dad about us kids but he didn't even try to hide his pride when Dad told him how well my GCSEs had gone.

'So, what are you going to do now?' He looked me in the eye as he asked the question. Dad had been right when he said that they looked alike. They definitely had the same eyes. People have always said that I had my dad's eyes but I try not to think about that one too much because I feel like I could drive myself insane. I mean yes, I have my dad's eyes but are they my dad's eyes or my uncle's? Strictly speaking my dad is my uncle and my uncle is my dad. Told you it's enough to drive you crazy.

Anyway, to get back to the question he'd asked. 'Art college,' I said, 'like my dad.' I couldn't stop myself from adding that bit on the end. I made sure that my eyes didn't move from his as I said it.

He nodded his head slowly. 'To do what?'

I felt like asking him what the hell it had to do with him but good manners stopped me and I told him. 'Graphic design.' I got the impression from the look on his face that he didn't think that was a proper subject, not one that would lead to a proper job anyway. Shows what he knows because I've done all right for myself, thank you very much.

Dad and Rob might not have had a lot to say each other that afternoon, but Grand-dad said even less. Now and again I would see him looking at his eldest son but I don't remember him saying anything. Gran on the other hand, well, you couldn't shut her up. She was asking him about the pub and she was all over Angie like a rash. To be fair to her she was probably only trying to make up for lost time but back then I was just a kid and I didn't see it that way.

Angie talked to Michael and Anthony about what they liked to do at school and stuff like that but she didn't say much to me. Rob didn't either come to that, not after the graphic design thing anyway. Not that it bothered me.

The conversation was pretty full on for a while, but it started to tail off after an hour or so and not long after that

Rob made noises about going.

'We need to get back before the Saturday night rush starts,' Angie said and it sounded like she was apologising.

Gran stood up to see them off but Rob ignored her and went to Dad. He held his hand out and Dad took it. 'Your sons are a credit to you, Tom,' he said. 'All of them.'

Dad thanked him.

The fact that he'd said all three of them wasn't lost on me and I guessed that he'd decided that he didn't want anything to do with me after all. Mum said later that he probably realised that I thought of his brother as my dad, but I wasn't so sure. Would the man that they had described to me give up so easily? Well he could sod off because I didn't want anything to do with him anyway.

Once Gran had seen them off she came back into the living room and smiled.

'That was nice wasn't it,' she said, but nobody said anything either way.

Uncle Craig came to see us the following day.

I was at the top of the stairs about to come down when Mum opened the door to him. He didn't see me as he focused his attention on his sister. They hugged each other.

'Are you all right?' he asked. Mum might have said something but I didn't hear it. Uncle Craig caught sight of me at that point and asked me the same question.

'Yeah, I'm fine,' I told him and then asked, 'You?'

He gave a non-committal shrug of the shoulders by way of a reply.

Dad appeared at the living room door and he went through the same routine that I had with Uncle Craig. The three of them disappeared into the kitchen and I went into the room Dad had left my brothers in. They were watching cricket on one of the sports channels.

They say that they used to be really good friends, but Uncle Craig wasn't pleased to see his mate return. When we were little Mum and Dad used to talk about when they were younger and there'd been stories of how Uncle Craig had got into fights to protect his little sister. I couldn't help thinking that if it came to The Battle of the Uncles it wouldn't end well for Rob. I knew who my money would be on anyway. It never has come to that but I think that's down to Mum persuading her brother not to rock the boat.

Anyway, once Rob and Angie had gone home, life got back to normal. I started Art College as planned, Anthony helped Michael to find his feet at secondary school and Mum and Dad carried on being our parents. It was the only thing that could happen really.

We didn't tell my brothers the truth for a long time. There didn't seem much point at first because nothing had changed in terms of my relationship with them – they were still my brothers just like they always had been – but then there reached a point where we thought, why not? It wasn't like it was going to change anything.

They took it in their stride, just like I'd known they would, and I got the impression that they wondered why we had even bothered. Nothing changed: I was still the big brother that I had always been.

In the years since that first meeting, despite what Dad feared, Rob has never mentioned that he is my biological father. Dad always says that he can't understand it. He says that maybe his brother has changed but he also says that he wouldn't trust him as far as he could throw him.

Perhaps they hadn't needed to tell me about what he actually is to me after all, but I'm glad that they did. If anything, I love them more than ever because of it. They, especially Dad, risked so much by telling me the truth. My mum was always going to be my mum but he risked me turning my back on him, risked me telling him that he wasn't my dad so he couldn't do anything. He told me that he didn't want me hearing it from Rob and had risked everything to avoid that.

My dad is an amazing man.

We see Rob and Angie a couple of times a year and, to be honest, that's enough for me.

We're seeing them today in fact. We normally meet up at Gran's house but we're going to them this time which makes a change. Today is a special occasion. He and Angie are getting married. I don't know why they're bothering, I mean they've been together for more than twenty years.

Dad's going to be his best man.

'Who else would I ask?' Rob had said when Dad asked him if he was sure there was no one else that he would rather ask. 'You're the one person I can rely on. You're my brother.'

RIBBONS IN HER HAIR
Colette McCormick

Jean seems the perfect wife and mother but she struggles to love her daughters unconditionally.

When the youngest daughter, Susan, brings 'shame' on the family, Jean can think of only one response. She has to make the problem disappear.

Examining the divide between generations, between mothers and daughters, this emotionally charged novel asks whether we can ever truly understand another, however close our ties.

THINGS I SHOULD HAVE SAID AND DONE
Colette McCormick

Ellen has everything to live for, so when her life is cut short by a drunk driver running a red light she is unwilling to let go.

From the limbo that she now inhabits Ellen can only watch as her husband struggles as a single parent and her mother falls apart. That is until she realises that her daughter can be a link between the two worlds.

From beyond the grave there are things that Ellen can do to influence the life that she left behind.

Á

Proudly published by Accent Press

www.accentpress.co.uk